R.I.P. W

# R.I.P. When All is Said and Done

## By

## Mike Hourston

## PREFACE

Visit five exciting stories that explore the meaning of justice, the afterlife, revenge, days gone by, and the world as seen through the eyes of a poet.

Story One: When an old friend has been murdered, do you have an obligation to see that justice is done? And, do you know what that justice should look like? Follow Mike, Deacon, and the Professor in this search for big and small answers that begin in Middle America and reach a climax in an abandoned church school in Washington D.C.

Story Two: Jerry Sizemore and two of his friends encounter a spirit named Evelyn as they cut through the cemetery one summer night. She shares a message that impacts Jerry for the rest of his life.

Story Three: Jack Chase must choose between marriage to Carrie, or killing the thug that murdered his brother.

Story Four: Alice Hoffmann explores a broken down mansion where she spent fifty years working as a servant. Along the way she runs into two young men in search of hidden treasure. They spend the afternoon together searching and reflecting on life.

Story Five: Follow Marty as he searches for a poem and what a poet is or should be.

R.I.P. When All is Said and Done

Copyright@ Mike Hourston

This is a work of fiction. Names, characters, and incidents depicted in these stories are products of the author's imagination and are used fictitiously. Any resemblance to actual events, or persons living or dead, is entirely coincidental and beyond the intent of the author.

# CONTENTS

STORY ONE ................................................................... 1

STORY TWO ................................................................. 70

STORY THREE ............................................................. 108

STORY FOUR ............................................................... 136

STORY FIVE ................................................................. 157

## STORY ONE

# New Times Meet Old Times

A hot, humid spring breeze carried the smell of fresh-cut grass as pallbearers Deacon, Mike, Gary, and Steve, dressed in black suits and bright-blue ties, watched the coffin of their murdered friend lowered into the ground at the big Catholic cemetery in Saint Louis.

Founded in 1854, Calvary held such luminaries as civil war general Sherman, and playwright Tennessee Williams. Today it welcomed its newest resident, at the age of fifty-two. The headstone, purchased by his friends, read *Bobby Aherne—Friend.*

After leading the small group in prayer, Deacon scattered a handful of earth over the coffin, and walked to a nearby maple tree. He gazed at the bustling traffic on Broadway Boulevard and realized all that separated those out there from God's eternity was the cemetery's six-foot cast-iron fence and one-hundred feet of pretty green grass. He wondered why life was often short and tragic.

Mike approached Deacon. "We can't let them get away with this. We owe Bobby."

Deacon rubbed away a tear, as he leaned against the tree. "I remembered us being young. We rode the bus to school, played baseball, camped and fished in those hot Saint Louis summers. And that sweet cotton candy and crazy red roller coaster at Fun Fair Park. I'm sure we got mad and miserable at times, yet we always had our tomorrows."

Deacon glanced at the grave. "Let's get something to eat and figure this out."

Walking to their cars, they noticed a short, plump, gray-haired man with a handlebar mustache standing next to a silver sedan.

Deacon asked, "Anybody know him?"

"Wow, dig the crazy black derby and gold chain and pocket watch. I've never seen a lavender bowtie—very dapper," Mike said.

"Sure, dapper a hundred years ago."

The old man, with the help of a cane, limped toward Bobby's gravesite, while three police cars—red-lights flashing—entered the cemetery followed by a hearse, ten limousines, and a long line of cars.

Mike watched the death procession pass and was reminded "nightfall" catches up with everyone—even big shots.

Deacon, Mike, Steve, and Gary arrived at Pete's diner around eleven-thirty. Most of the seats were empty.

Pete's Place had been serving hamburgers, pizza, fries, and other short-order items for over forty years, and was the last diner left in the neighborhood. Owners Pete and Mary Carlyle, now in their late seventies, worked every day. Pete, in overalls and gray sweatshirt, was in the kitchen. Mary, always in a dress, served tables and managed the cash register.

Mike headed toward a window booth in the back. "Let's grab our spot."

The wooden tables and chairs were original and worn. The booths' green upholstery had patches. Scuffs, scratches and cracks covered the gray tiled floor. Other than prices, the menu hadn't changed since the place opened.

Mary stared for a moment, and then hurried over. "I haven't seen you boys in years. Steve, you used to be thin. And Deacon, you've gotten so gray."

She patted Deacon on the back. "Pete will be glad to see you guys. I guess it's the usual?"

"You bet."

Mary scanned the table. "Hey, what's with those black suits and blue ties, and where's the other member of your crew, Bobby?"

Deacon looked up. "We buried him at Calvary an hour ago."

Mary grabbed a chair and scooted up to the booth. "Oh my God! How, where, when did this happen?"

"Someone murdered him. The D.C. cops told me he'd been beaten—maybe tortured, and then shot."

"What was he doing in Washington?"

"We don't know—yet. Bobby had me listed as contact person on the back of his driver's license, so the D.C. cops called me—a Sergeant Craft. I couldn't tell him anything useful. After they finished with the body, I had it shipped back here. Now he's at Calvary next to his mom and dad."

"Have the cops caught who did this?"

"Not so far."

Mary headed toward the kitchen. "I'll tell Pete."

## R.I.P. When All is Said and Done

Mike scanned the empty parking lot. "This place used to be packed at lunch time. Remember the jukebox over there in the corner. For a couple of summers all you heard was Beatles or Beach Boys music. I still listen to those guys."

Deacon took off his jacket. "I haven't been back in over twenty years. There are a couple of social media sites where people post and update the goings-on here. Seems the whole neighborhood has gone to hell. On the ride over you guys must have noticed how beat up things are. You know they had eight murders in the neighborhood last year."

Gary said, "Push hard enough and anything will topple. We moved to California after I graduated high school, and I haven't been back till now."

Steve nudged Mike as an old couple sat down. "That's Dave and Amy Shoults. You remember Dan Shoults from high school. Those are his parents. Dan ought to get them out before they get killed."

Mike asked, "What happens to Bobby's things?"

Deacon rolled his eyes. "What things? He lived in a trailer park way out on Bryan Road. I stopped there last week and rummaged around for some decent clothes he could be buried in. All I found was some old jeans, a few dirty plaid shirts, and a couple pairs of tennis shoes. Oh yes, there was a broken radio. The place was so messy it looked like it had been ransacked. Hell, I bought the suit we buried him in."

Steve pointed at the pack of cigarettes in Mike's shirt pocket. "I see you're still smoking."

"Two packs a day for thirty-five years. Bobby and I smoked our first cigarette together, and then Deacon a couple months later. I think we were twelve or thirteen. We could buy a pack for a quarter at the drug store, and no one asked us about our age."

Mary arrived pushing a small cart with a couple pitchers of draught beer, and two thin-crust, extra-large, three-topping (sausage, bacon, pepperoni) pizzas. "This is on the house. Wave when you guys are ready to leave and I'll bring Pete over."

Deacon and the others spent the next hour sharing stories and reminiscing. Their working-class neighborhood was built in the

Fifties. The tight little wood-frame ranch homes were eight- hundred square feet, with a single bathroom. You could buy one for ten-thousand dollars. Most mortgages were backed by the G.I. Bill, since the majority of applicants were veterans of WWII or Korea. In those days, moms stayed home raising a family of four or five kids, while dad worked at a factory, drove a truck, or repaired something. The Catholic, Baptist, and Presbyterian churches got filled on Sunday, and even the public schools did OK. Packed with kids, the neighborhood was safe and friendly. Lawns were cut, flowers planted, and weeds pulled. Every back yard had a clothesline where moms hung white sheets and other items that fluttered in the spring and summer winds. Ten walking minutes from anywhere in the neighborhood was that strip mall with its Ben Franklin dime store, drug store, mom-and-pop grocery, little bakery, a barber shop with three chairs, and next to it a girl's dance studio. Kids bought penny candy, models, comic books, or just hung out there. It had a doctor's office in the back; he even made house calls.

They shared baseball, fishing, and camping memories. First girlfriends—the names Karen and Leslie came up. And favorite old coaches—Pete had coached their little league baseball team for four years.

Mike glanced at the parking lot. "I'll be damned, that old pine tree is still hanging on. It looked half-dead when we were kids. We fought those guys from Dellwood near that tree. Bobby waded into them and bloodied that big kid's nose and they went running. Nothing scared him."

Mike raised his glass. "Let's give it up for Bobby."

After the toast, Deacon said, "Somebody from around here posted pictures of the strip mall on the Internet showing all the buildings boarded up, and then a big empty lot after the bulldozers knocked and hauled everything away. My grandma bought me my first comic book at the dime store. She lived with us till she passed. Everybody called her Nanny. She was feisty, and you better not mess with her grandson—me. We had her funeral mass at St. Pius, and now she's buried out at Calvary not far from Bobby. Steve, she used to baby sit you."

"I remember Nanny—a sweet old lady. She would be spinning in her grave if she heard what's happened to the neighborhood."

"Then let's not tell her."

Mike grabbed the second pitcher and refilled everyone's glass. "Used-to-be times are the only worthwhile times left around here."

Deacon slapped the table. "We can't save Bobby or the neighborhood, but we can get those responsible for killing Bobby."

They stared at each other, and then the conversation shifted to what they had been doing since they left the neighborhood.

Deacon, real name Joe Gannon, had gotten an MBA from the University of Missouri, and then spent the next thirty years working at an investment bank in New York. Retired, he and his wife Kathy lived in Buffalo, New York.

Mike Lipton, enlisted in the Army right after high school, fought in both Gulf Wars, received two bronze stars and a purple heart. After twenty years he left the service with the rank of Sergeant. Divorced, he lived in Madison, Wisconsin, and did contract work in the security field.

Steve Klein, a diabetic, worked as a delivery driver for a large grocery chain in California.

Gary Smith had worked in the construction field. After an accident injured his shoulder, he went on disability and hadn't worked in over ten years. He lived alone in Bakersfield, California.

Mike shoved twenty dollars under a plate, while Deacon signaled Mary they were leaving.

Pete, thin, bald and bent over, shook hands; Mary gave everyone a smile and a hug.

Pete looked at Deacon. "This Sunday we'll drive over to Calvary and visit Bobby."

"He would like that."

"Have you guys got anything planned the rest of the day?"

"We've decided to spend a few hours riding around revisiting old sites to see how bad things have gotten."

Pete leaned against the counter. "The neighborhood has been bleeding to death for years. The state took over running the local public school district. St. Pius, the Catholic grade school, closed fifteen years ago. Seven years ago the archdiocese pulled the priest and shuttered the church. The buildings are still over there on Shepley—sort of. Crime is way up, and property values way down.

"We still live on Lancashire, but have metal bars on the front and back doors. Last summer an immigrant from Latvia got robbed and killed while selling ice cream on our street."

"Jesus, Pete, do whatever you have to do to get out."

Pete glanced over at Mary. "We're trapped in this rubble. Houses are selling for what it cost to build them back in the Fifties, and my business has been losing money for years. I had a bout with lung cancer a few years back and we still owe on that. We don't have much put away, and don't want to be a burden to our kids. Tom lives in Seattle, and been out of work for over a year. Cathy's a Franciscan nun helping other people in Beaverton, Oregon. I ought to close and move West across the river and try and get us a small apartment."

After several more hugs and handshakes, Deacon and the others headed to the parking lot and gathered around Mike's ten-year old dusty-gray F-150 truck.

Steve shook his head. "Mary wore that same red dress thirty years ago. She's so pale and thin. Her skin hangs on her bones. And did you notice those bloodshot eyes."

Mike opened the truck door. "Her and Pete are old, broke, and have no place to go. They're worn out and worried. When they're gone, like the neighborhood, they'll leave the world unremembered."

Deacon glanced back at the diner. "Despite all that's happened, Mary still has that great smile. You guys saw it. Bless her, she's special. She reminds me a lot of my mom."

Mike started up the engine. "Let's see how bad things have gotten."

With Mike behind the wheel, they pulled onto Spring Garden Drive.

Gary tapped Mike on the shoulder. "Let's check out my old place."

Deacon pointed as they drove past Mike's boarded-up house. "Remember all the penny ante poker we played in your basement—even on school nights."

"Oh yeah, and my mom and dad never complained about the noise. They put up with a lot. Dad served three years in the South Pacific during World War II. He and mom are buried at Jefferson Barracks military cemetery. They and others like them made this neighborhood great."

They got halfway down Grampian Drive and stopped.

Gary stared out the window. "It's gone."

A couple of kids on bikes told them Gary's old house had burned down over a year ago.

Gary got out and kicked the ground and cursed as he came across a rusted-out wagon, an old hammer, and other debris.

After a few minutes, Gary jumped back in the truck. "Let's get out of here."

"Let's head over to St. Pius. It's closed, but Pete says the buildings are still there," Deacon said.

Five minutes later they pulled into a parking lot of broken clumps of asphalt and foot-high weeds. Mike maneuvered around potholes and splinters of glass, and parked. Forty years ago, hundreds of kids laughed and hollered playing kick ball and tag on this black top, girls running and jumping in their light-green school uniforms, boys in their white shirts and blue slacks. An hour of fun every day—till the bell rang. Hair styles included lots of curls and home permanents for the girls, while guys had crew cuts and flat tops. A boy with one hair hanging over his ear would be sent home. Now half the windows in the school were cracked or broken.

Mike pointed at the rectory where a fire had left the roof caved in. "Three priests lived there. Remember good old Father Hederman. After every confession, to get right with the Lord, he made us pray three Our Fathers and ten Hail Mary's. He was tough. I heard he later got upped to Monsignor. The Franciscan nuns stayed at the building next to it. This place had twelve nuns teaching in those days, counting Sister Tarsilla the principal. At least their building hasn't burned down—yet."

Deacon said, "This was a good school. I wouldn't trade the experience for anything. How about you guys?"

Steve lowered the back window. "Something good they let die. You guys want to leave, or stay and hold your nose?"

Mike opened the door, hesitated for a moment, and then got out. "Let's look around."

The steel door near the first grade rooms was ajar.

Steve kicked the broken metal padlock lying next to the door. "I was a hall monitor in the seventh and eighth grades."

They entered the first room on the right. A small wooden desk remained in the middle of the room. Rocks, pitched through several windows, lay strewn on the cracked tile floor.

Mike studied a thick patch of black goo clinging to the back wall where the bookshelves used to be. "Let's not stay too long."

Deacon observed. "We learned the alphabet in this room, and the first word I could spell was Y E L L O W. God knows why I remember that. I guess when you're a kid little achievements make you feel so good. Funny, how big it seemed at the time."

Mike stared at the blackboard where someone had spray painted F U C K   Y O U   in bright red. "Sister didn't teach us to spell that, but it sums things up around here."

Gary rubbed the back of his head. "How many times do you guys figure we got smacked in this room by good old Sister Annunciata? She was scary coming at you in that black Franciscan outfit. Even my mom and dad were afraid of her."

Mike laughed, and said, "You never knew when she was going to draw and fire those big hands. And the girls got it as often as the guys. She pounded the hell out of everybody in the dumb row, particularly Greg and Terry. Didn't she flunk those two idiots?"

"Yeah, they flunked. The next year their parents sent them to the public school, and they never flunked again. Even in those days public schools were more tolerant of idiots."

Mike strolled to the front of the room. "This is where Sister had you kneel, book in each hand with arms outstretched. I wonder where she learned that torture."

Deacon peered out the window. "I sat in the row nearest these windows and gazed at the soccer fields and those woods behind the fields. When I wasn't being a great soccer player, I dreamed I was in those woods fighting Indians to save the neighborhood."

Mike surveyed the room. "Indians didn't do this."

A shaggy brown rodent with a long thick tail scurried across the floor.

Mike watched the rat disappear in a corner hole. "Let's head over to the church and see what they left there." He smashed a big black spider crawling up the wall as he headed out the door.

The old church doors were locked so they peeked through the cracked and broken windows. Benches, candles, chairs, holy water, and statues of Saints Joseph and Mary were gone, along with the altar. Nothing hinted this building had represented a Catholic church, or church of any kind.

Deacon glanced up. "They've even removed the cross atop the building. They don't fool around when they decommission God's house."

Mike leaned against the door. "I remember marching in there for First Communion, the boys in white shirts, ties, and blue slacks, and the girls in their snow-white dresses. The next year we paraded in for Confirmation to become Soldiers for Christ. I sang and did altar boy duty in there."

Deacon said, "At Christmas, the nuns set the manger to the left of the altar, and surrounded it with four or five short-needle pine trees wrapped with strings of dark-blue lights. My mom and I would arrive way early for Sunday services to get a pew close to the manger. After mass we gazed at the manger, those bright lights, and inhaled those rich pine smells for a few more minutes before leaving. I think about that every Christmas. Until she died my mom would always call and remind me of a coming holy day. You know, making sure I attended mass that day. I've missed a few since she's been gone. Shame on me—I can do better."

Mike said, "We prayed a lot of Hail Mary's and Our Father's in there. None of our parents had much, yet they faithfully dropped their hard-earned cash in those collection baskets every Sunday while we wore hand-me-down clothes with patches. Hell, patches on patches. Makes you wonder if anything of real importance ever occurred here."

Deacon took off his tie. "God knows."

"I wish He would make it a little bit clearer. I don't need a voice from a burning bush, but maybe something other than an abandoned church and burnt out rectory to help keep me going. You know what I mean."

Deacon wrapped his tie around the large door handle of the former church. Mike followed with his tie, and then Gary and Steve. Deacon had suggested they all wear blue ties, because blue was Bobby's favorite color.

Gary finished his knot. "Let's get the fuck out of this junkyard before the neighborhood demons show up."

"At least the sun still shines around here," Deacon said.

Mike lit a cigarette as he walked away. "All it shines on is bugs, rats, and broken shit."

## The Professor

Mike gestured as they headed back to the parking lot. "Hey, it's that old guy with the cane and black derby we saw at the cemetery. I wonder what the hell he wants."

The old man introduced himself as Stephen Mason, retired philosophy professor from the University of Missouri. He lived off Hanley Road in the city of Clayton, a small wealthy community about twenty miles away.

Deacon asked, "Professor Mason, what's on your mind?"

In a calm voice, the Professor said, "The people who killed your friend Bobby must be held accountable."

"What was Bobby to you?"

"I hired him to check out something in Washington, and it cost his life. I won't leave it there."

Mike turned to Deacon. "Bobby was doing that kind of work?"

Deacon nodded. "About six months ago, after getting laid off at the steel plant, Bobby mentioned in an email he was thinking about being a private detective. I guess he thought it would be fun and exciting. You know Bobby."

Deacon asked, "What was he working on that got him killed?"

"We were checking into stuff maybe connected to a big-shot politician in Washington. I'm going to get justice for Bobby. Would you guys be interested in working with me on this?"

Mike didn't hesitate. "I'm doing something with or without you."

Gary and Steve glanced at each other, while Deacon leaned against the truck.

The Professor handed Mike his business card. "Call me whatever you guys decide."

The Professor glanced back as he opened the door of his silver Mercedes. "To make things better people need to give a shit, and then act. We can meet and I'll fill you in on what I know, and discuss the next step."

After Professor Mason drove away, Gary said, "Why should we get involved with that old guy? Bobby got killed working with him.

Besides, the cops are investigating who killed Bobby, and the political stuff is none of our fucking business."

Steve agreed. "There's nothing we can do about what happened. We buried Bobby, let's leave it there."

Mike pounded the hood of his truck. "I'm not going to let the bastards get away with this, and I don't care if big shots are involved."

Deacon stared at the school, and then the rectory. "I have to call my wife, but I'll stay and see what this guy has to say."

Gary jumped in the back seat of the truck. "I can't, I've done enough flying down here for the funeral. Bobby would understand."

Steve shook hands with Mike and Deacon. "I got to get back to California. My grown kids are living with us, and my job doesn't pay shit. I can't afford to take off, not even for Bobby."

They rode back to Pete's parking lot, and wished each other luck.

Mike turned to Deacon, as Steve and Gary drove off. "Everybody has their fucking excuses. I'll give this Professor a call, and we can set up a time and place to meet."

Deacon agreed. "That old guy is worth a listen. Let's run his name on the Internet and see if anything pops up. If it doesn't feel right, we'll go at this on our own."

Wednesday morning, after dropping off his rental, Deacon rode with Mike to their ten o'clock meeting with Professor Mason at Ottoman's Coffee House, located in the outer suburbs of St. Louis.

About nine-fifty, Mike pulled off Bircher Avenue and found a place to park at the far end of the lot next to the nature preserve. The Professor's car was in a handicap space near the door.

Built as a hunting lodge way back in 1923, the story-and-a-half gray-stone structure had been converted to a coffee house in the Nineties. The renovations retained the rustic feel, the scuffed hardwood floors had been refinished, and the dark paneled walls re-stained. Ottoman's was known for its strong coffees and fresh-baked apple, cherry, and pecan pies, and sugar-coated pastries. Sweet scents and fresh-brewed aromas spilled into the parking area, acting as a magnet to hurry people in.

Six large ceiling fans spun over the vaulted first floor. On the walls hung portraits of Shelley, Poe, Socrates, Hubble, Einstein, Curie, and many others. A reminder of humanity's potential for greatness. Servers pushed their carts down a path in the center of the room. Ottoman's seated one hundred-twenty, and was always open.

Mike and Deacon, in jeans and sweatshirts, spotted Professor Mason at a small wooden table next to a window. He was wearing a gray pin-stripe suit with a green bowtie, and a welcoming smile on his puffy-red face.

The Professor extended his hand. "Nice to see you guys."

After they ordered, Mike scanned the crowded room. "It's so quiet in here."

"Sometimes the only thing you hear is the creaking sound from those old wood floor boards. That's part of the cozy charm of this place. It's all about quiet conversation, reading a book or magazine article, or meditating while enjoying a warm cup of coffee and eating a soft, fresh-baked sweet roll."

The Professor pointed to steps leading to the second floor. "There's a small library up there with bookshelves of poetry, novels, Greek and Roman histories, and other classics. You can relax and experience shared wisdom and inspired insights—if you want to.

I've re-read Keats' *Ode on a Grecian Urn* a dozen times. That Urn and Keats will live forever.

"A young gal named Liz spends a lot of time up there in the library reading Poe and Shelley. She told me she wants to be a poet. I wish her luck.

"You'll be warned, if you get too loud, or your cell phone goes off in here. The second time, you'll be told to leave. I'm here at seven in the morning, at least five days a week, reading, thinking, getting away from the noise and clutter out there, and dreaming a better world.

"You noticed the menu is coffee and pastries. If you want bacon and eggs, a porterhouse steak, or French fries—go somewhere else."

The Professor directed their attention to a table across the room. "See those six folks. Every Wednesday morning they arrive at eight o'clock in a brown station wagon, each carrying a book. The two gentlemen are always in suit and tie, and the four ladies in dresses, hair fixed real nice, and wearing jewelry. The guys seat the ladies, and then they order several platters of glazed donuts to go with their coffee. A year ago, I walked by and they were all holding copies of a Sherlock Holmes mystery. The next week they were reading Ray Chandler's *The Big Sleep*. They got to be in their eighties. I never see them with anyone else. You know, sons, daughters, grandkids. There used to be three guys until about six months ago."

The Professor stared for a moment. "I kind of feel sorry for them."

Pushing a tray, a tall, blond-haired young man arrived. He handed Mike a plate of three sugar-coated donuts bursting with dark-red jelly, and set two plump lemon sweet rolls in front of Deacon. After filling their sixteen-ounce coffee mugs, he left.

The Professor leaned toward Deacon. "That fruity aroma, it must be a terebinth coffee. It lifts you off the ground. Now that's coffee."

"I like it strong."

Mike turned off his cellphone. "Professor, I see you've been published. A book on Aristotle, and one about a guy I never heard of named Boethius."

"Boethius was a great man. Yet, except for a few scholars, his name is almost unknown today. I first read his *The Consolation of Philosophy*, while in graduate school out East. He produced that seminal work in the early sixth century A.D. while awaiting execution."

"We're all waiting to die."

The Professor tugged at his long gray mustache. "I can't imagine producing anything coherent knowing on such-and-such morning I would be taken somewhere to be tortured and killed. Boethius was made of stern stuff, a special man. What he shared all those centuries ago still supplies perspective about life's opportunities, challenges, and obligations. That's worth knowing, and thinking about. I've asked the owners to add his name with the other greats hanging on these walls."

"Now virtually no one knows or gives a shit about him or his little book. Makes you wonder if his work and death meant or means anything."

"That's a question everyone should ask. What you do with your life, and does it have meaning."

"I have faith it does," Deacon said.

The Professor raised his cup. "I agree. Whether you end up recognized on a wall or not, all this must have meaning.

Mike tossed his napkin on his plate. "Well then, here we are. Bobby's death had meaning, and what we're going to do about it will have meaning. Where do we go from there?"

Deacon stared across the table. "To start, the Professor is going to tell us what Bobby was doing in Washington, and who he thinks killed him."

The Professor grabbed his cane. "There's a path running through those woods. It's a nice day, let's walk and talk."

The Professor picked up the check, and Deacon and Mike took care of the tip.

## Of Gnats and Men

Deacon and the Professor crossed the asphalt lot while Mike ran to his truck and grabbed his .38 caliber handgun. He shoved it inside his belt, covering it with his shirt, and caught up with the others as they reached the edge of the parking lot.

The Professor pointed his cane at a narrow dirt path lying between two large snowball bushes about thirty feet away.

Deacon gazed at the path. "Are you sure you're up to this? We can sit in the truck and talk."

The Professor stepped forward. "I've been over that path hundreds of times. Let's go."

Deacon and the Professor walked side-by-side on the tight five-foot wide path, as the mid-day sun poked through the thick canopy of leafy oaks and maples. Mike followed a few steps behind, checking the woods as they went.

They paused to enjoy the woodsy fragrance coming from a patch of sweet sunflowers.

The Professor held his hand next to his ear. "You can hear the quiet whispers of our friends the honeybees hard at work on a warm spring day—if you listen."

After swatting a mosquito, the Professor brushed back a low hanging tree limb with his cane as they continued along the path. "I only knew Bobby for a short while, but I liked and respected him. The guy was smart, gutsy, and nobody's fool. His death hurt, and I'm committed to right that wrong."

Deacon said, "The cop investigating this told me it appeared Bobby was tortured before being shot. He was strong as a bull. It would take more than one guy to bring him down. What or who was he investigating that got him killed? You mentioned something about a politician."

"The local papers and TV stations up there covered Bobby's death like one of those less than fifteen-minute stories. And I don't know how interested the cops are in solving this. I think they wish someone would come in and confess so they could close the books on this."

The Professor stopped to rest where a log had fallen. Large oaks provided shade; at eighty-two degrees the temperature was beginning to feel uncomfortable. He eased himself on the log, and then set his cane by his side. Mike dodged a passing wasp, and then sat next to the Professor. Deacon stood and planted his right foot on the log, and leaned toward the Professor.

The Professor set his derby in his lap, and pulled from his back pocket a small flask filled with a sweet flavored orange liquid.

After taking a drink, he wiped his sweaty brow. "Three months ago, I was in Washington attending a symposium on Aristotle. Even retired, I like attending those events. I once traveled to Athens. It's fun to talk to folks in your field and discuss new interpretations and insights on our greatest philosopher.

"I took time to visit the planetarium at Rock Creek Park, and later strolled along its wooded trails."

The Professor held out the flask. "It's an energy drink. You boys want a sip?"

They turned his offer down, and the Professor continued. "After walking a while, I eased myself on to a soft, grassy area off the trail, and lay down. Resting—not sleeping. About ten minutes passed, and then I hear a slight rustling sound. I raised myself up a little and peeked through the thick brush. I saw a thin Asian man in jeans and black turtleneck sweater shoving a thick plastic envelope under a juniper bush about thirty feet off the trail. He glanced around, got back to the trail, and then headed north in a hurry. I lay there trying to figure out what that was all about when an attractive blonde in her late teens or early twenties comes running up in a blue sweatshirt, gray sweatpants, and white tennis shoes. She headed straight to the juniper bush and opened the envelope. She pulled out a fistful of cash, stared at it for a second, and then put it back in the envelope. Then she shoved the envelope in her backpack and took off running south on the trail. I used my phone to snap a picture of her holding that big wad of cash. From the time she arrived to the time she left was less than two minutes."

Mike nudged the Professor. "Man, you got an eye for detail."

The Professor stretched out his legs. "What did I have other than a photograph of an attractive young woman in the woods holding a fistful of cash? Sure, it might be a ransom payoff, or a hundred other things. Was she in charge of whatever this was, or was there someone important behind her? And who was the tough-looking Asian character? There were a lot of questions, with no answers. I had a damn picture and my imagination—maybe running wild."

With the aid of Deacon, the Professor rose, and pointed. "A little past that stand of poplar trees the path circles a beautiful lake. It's ten minutes from here."

They walked about twenty feet, when the Professor turned to Deacon. "You're wondering why I should have cared. Whether the whole thing was innocent or dirty—that's Washington."

"That thought crossed my mind."

"I wondered myself. I attended a few more presentations, took in the sights, and then flew back to St. Louis. At home, I printed the photo and hung it on my office wall and stared at it for hours over a couple of days. I even had a dream about that Asian guy and her. I don't have kids, and since my wife died I've wanted to do something that could create meaning out of what is left of my time. A picture of a gal holding a wad of cash was going to be my place to start."

Movement in the bushes ahead on the left caused Mike to pull out his .38, and aim in the direction of the sound. A moment later, a doe with a couple of fawns bolted up the steep grassy hill, then disappeared into a stand of pear trees.

Mike shoved the gun back inside his belt. "I guess we'll let them go."

The Professor asked. "What are you prepared for?"

"Anything."

"You're a smart man."

Tracking over thick grass and weeds, they disturbed a swarm of gnats.

Mike swung at the swirling dots, while Deacon mused, "I read gnats survive for a few weeks—if they're lucky. I wonder if it's a life worth living. Or if they can be happy?"

The Professor thought a moment. "I don't know whether they can be happy, wise, or witty, but they have a job to do, otherwise they wouldn't be here. Like us, they have to make the most of the life they get. That I'm sure of."

They cut through a patch of evergreens and arrived at the lake; eight acres of spring-fed clear water, with depths ranging from a couple of feet up to ten. Here the path tightened, hemmed in by thick underbrush and maple and oak trees pushing their limbs over the water's edge.

The Professor glanced toward a small cove. "Let's hike over there."

At the cove, the Professor sat on a rotting tree stump about ten feet from where the lake lapped up against its bank. Deacon and Mike shared a fallen log nearby.

The Professor gazed at the lake. "Deer and duck stands were all around when this was owned by the hunting lodge. Folks stayed for the weekend, popped away, and then headed back. They tell me the lake is full of bass, catfish, and bluegill. I've never seen any fishermen, and only a few hikers. The woods are now a preserve, no hunting allowed. I used to come here and read poetry with my wife Clemmy. She loved wildflowers, particularly those purple asters. You guys would have liked her.

"See the oak tree near that big rock, its thick leafy branches jutting out over the lake. I've watched it double in size. We're growing older together. The last three years, the same pair of cardinals has raised a family of chicks in its branches. I've named them Herschel and Clementine. I always wave and wish them well. They recognize me. You'll see when we walk under the tree on our way out."

The Professor glanced at Deacon. "You mentioned happiness. It's all around."

Mike flung a rock into the lake. "Can we get back to the photo you took up in Washington?"

"Sorry, I tend to lose myself out here. By all means, let's discuss the photo, what happened, and where we go from here.

"I needed to talk to that young gal in the photograph. Maybe she would provide a plausible reason for the curious way of picking up cash. Also, she might be able to tell me about the fellow who delivered the cash. I didn't have his picture so I hired a local artist to create a sketch based on my description. It came out pretty well.

"I thought about posting her photo and the sketch out on social media. The problem was it might alert them if they were up to no good. Plus, a public shout-out would trace back to me. I didn't know how much risk there might be, and didn't want to take too many chances till I had a better sense of things. So, I decided to go old-school. Visit bars, nightclubs, and other private and public venues, and show her photo and that sketch around to see if anybody recognized them. You know, burn a lot of shoe leather and see what shakes loose—if anything."

The Professor scooted off the tree stump and stretched his arms upward. "My plan needed fresh legs and more energy than I got. That's where Bobby came in. I responded to his ad in a local paper offering Discrete Investigations. I hired him, and two and a half months ago, we met at the coffee shop and planned our strategy.

"We didn't want anyone to know we were together, so we drove to Washington in separate cars, and stayed at different motels. We also decided there would be no electronic communication between us, no electronic trail leading to the other. If this blew up, one of us would have a better chance of getting out of there. That precaution might have saved my life.

"Bobby updated me in person. We first met at the planetarium. From there we set up the next time and place to meet, and so on.

"Bobby asked bartenders, waitresses, doorman, and others if they recognized the gal in the photo, or the guy in the sketch. He spent two afternoons in the park where the drop-off took place, stopping joggers and others. After a couple of weeks, he got a hit on the girl. A doorman working at Barnacle's, a fancy nightclub in the Foggy Bottom area of Washington, recognized her. Bobby learned she stopped by Thursday evenings with a group."

The Professor reached out to Mike. "Can I borrow a smoke?"

"Sure."

After Mike lit his cigarette, the Professor continued. "That Thursday, Bobby waited at the bar and me at a table. Around seven-thirty, a group of five ladies came in, and one of them matched the girl in the photo. I used my phone to take a bunch of pictures. First, to make sure this was the right girl. If she was, we'd also have photos of her friends. Never know where that might lead. After fifteen or so minutes a couple of young guys joined the others. I took more photos, and drank. Bobby stayed at the bar. The real money shot arrived a little after nine o'clock."

The Professor dropped his cane, and then eased himself back on the tree stump. "An attractive, middle-aged woman arrived with an older, well-dressed gentleman. The woman chatted with the group, hugged the young gal we were focused on, and then she and her companion entered a private room in the back. That woman was Teresa Hodge, senior senator from Oregon, and presidential candidate. At her side was U.S. Attorney General James Kidd. How's that for a power couple.

"A couple of days later Bobby and I strolled around the zoo, piecing together what we had. A check of Senator Hodge's on-line site revealed our young gal as an intern on the senator's staff named Rebecca Townsend, in her senior year at Georgetown University. Her dad worked for a big investment bank, and her parents lived in Manhattan.

"We figured Rebecca was the key to unlocking whatever this might be. We needed to find out about the cash picked up that day, and maybe other days. And, was she doing it for the senator, or someone else? We didn't think this was her game. Hell, she's barely more than a kid. We now knew where she worked, so the plan was for Bobby to follow her movements until he could catch her alone and hand her that picture of her holding the cash. On the back of the picture, I had written, *We Know What's Going On.* Underneath that succinct statement, we put Bobby's burner phone number. We didn't know shit, but needed to shake things up.

"We found where she lived. One morning, as she headed from her apartment to her car, Bobby ran up, shoved the picture at her, and took off. And then we waited. We had no leads on our Asian guy. So if she didn't call within a week, we were going to send the photo and how it might tie to the senator to a tabloid, and let them run with it if they wanted to."

The Professor squeezed his cigarette out between his thumb and forefinger, and then placed the butt in his shirt pocket. "Two days later, on a Sunday afternoon, Bobby gets a call from a gal claiming to be Rebecca. She wanted to meet and explain the photo in a public place—she suggested the Washington Monument. They set the time at noon Tuesday. To help identify him, she asked Bobby to wear a white shirt with a red rose in his lapel."

Deacon shook his head. "I don't know. I think I would have insisted on meeting at her apartment, or maybe a bar. A white shirt and red rose hung like a bullseye on Bobby. Anybody wanting to do him harm would have no trouble spotting him."

"I didn't like the setup, but your friend Bobby didn't spook. He figured nobody would try something there at high noon. Plus, he was anxious to move this along."

Mike grinned, and said, "That's our Bobby, 'Give me the fucking ball and let's go. That red-headed son-of-a bitch was special."

The Professor watched a small gray fox bolt past in pursuit of a cottontail. "If the rabbit escapes, the fox loses. If the fox wins the race, the rabbit loses. Either way, they're lucky if they survive a few terrifying years. It doesn't seem fair to either."

After the fox and rabbit zig-zagged and disappeared into a patch of blueberries, Mike quipped, "Who knows what fair is. Folks have been fighting about that for a long time. Nature has figured it out. Be the fittest or lose the race. That's all that counts."

The Professor glanced at Deacon, and continued. "I got there an hour ahead of Bobby, took pictures, acted like a tourist, and checked for anything that seemed strange or out of place. I'm an amateur at all this. Somebody slick could have been there and I wouldn't have noticed them. Anyway, Bobby arrived in a cab, and hung around the Monument, red rose and all, for about two hours. The gal never showed. Bobby left, and I watched to see if anyone followed him. The next afternoon, we met at *Ivies*, an out-of-the-way bar and grill near Kingman Park.

"She not showing up bothered us. Bobby changed cabs a couple of times on the way back to his hotel. We drank and talked, and decided to go to her apartment and confront her. We still didn't know what we had, but hoped we were making people nervous.

"Anyway, Bobby got no answer at her apartment, and found out from a neighbor she hadn't been seen for several days. Bobby then gets a call from this Rebecca on his burner phone. She claimed there had been a mix up about the time they were supposed to meet, and could they still get together. She suggested Saturday evening at seven o'clock outside Ford's Theater, and then head to a nearby restaurant where they could have a public-private discussion.

"I didn't trust her, and had a bad feeling about the setup, but we went ahead. I got there at six o'clock, and stationed myself across the street. Bobby arrived in a cab right at seven, lit a cigarette, and waited. Around ten after seven she showed, and I got a picture of them together. After a couple of minutes they headed down $10^{th}$ Street in the direction of McSweeneys, about five blocks away. I mixed in with the heavy pedestrian traffic, trying to stay out of sight while keeping them in view. I don't move fast enough these days, and within a few minutes they got a block ahead of me, and then I lost sight of them. I got to McSweeneys and didn't see Bobby or the girl. I figured they went in, so I hung out front, glancing in the window, trying to spot their table. After fifteen minutes, I went in and described them to the hostess. She told me no one fitting their description had come in. I walked around, didn't see them, and left. Bobby wouldn't have gone past the restaurant, so I backtracked to an alley a block before you get to the restaurant. I couldn't figure how she got him down there, yet that's where they must have snatched him."

Mike stomped out his cigarette. "Bobby was a tough dude. It would have taken two of three guys to take him down."

"I agree. They probably injected him with a drug, and then shoved him in a waiting car. Late the next day, I heard on the news Bobby's body was found near the Arlington Bridge."

Deacon nodded. "Sergeant Bill Craft told me the autopsy showed propofol in his system. That would do it. Also, he indicated Bobby was covered with cuts, burns, and bruises. However, a bullet through the heart killed him. I gave him the address of the funeral home to ship the body to, and haven't talked to him since."

The Professor said, "After I learned of Bobby's death, I called the cops on my burner phone and told them Bobby was with Rebecca Townsend that night. I mailed them a copy of the picture I took of them in front of Ford's Theater. I also suggested, over the phone, maybe Senator Hodge might know something. I didn't give the cops my name. A few days later, I called back and talked with that Sergeant Craft you mentioned. All he told me was the body would be shipped to St. Louis in a couple of weeks or so. He tried to pump me for more information, but I held back. I intended on returning to Washington and make things right. I read the announcement of the funeral, and drove out to Calvary to pay my respects. I saw you guys and figured you would be interested in doing something about this."

Mike glanced up as a flock of thirty or so Mallards circled and then descended on the lake, quacking and pounding the water a hundred yards away. "Those 'greenheads' are lucky they don't allow hunting around here anymore. Timing can be everything. I had a great aunt who died of tuberculosis at nineteen. Ten years later they had drugs to fight that disease. Some things work that way, and you can't do anything about it. With Bobby it's different—we can do something."

The Professor spotted a white plastic drinking cup floating near the water's edge, and shoved it in his back pocket.

Deacon asked, "Professor, why didn't you give the cops your name, and what you and Bobby were doing? It might help with their investigation."

"I figured they tortured Bobby to give up names. The only name he could have given them was my name. If I gave the cops my name, it would have got out and Bobby would have endured torture for nothing. Also, I'm not sure how much the D.C. cops want to pursue stuff involving political heavyweights. Hell, they might be in on whatever this might be. Right now I don't know who to trust. Maybe it's this Sergeant Craft. I will share everything and make everyone take notice after I've got dead-bang evidence against those who killed Bobby and the people behind all of this"

Mike slapped his hands together. "Let's get this started."

"Great, I need coffee. In a half-mile the path circles back and takes us to the parking lot."

Five minutes later, as they approached the Professor's favorite oak tree, two cardinals peered down from their busy nest and flapped their wings.

The Professor tipped his derby. "Herschel and Clementine are raising another wonderful family. Listen to their little ones cry for food."

Deacon and Mike looked up and waved. At this point, the dusty path widened allowing them to walk three abreast.

At the summit of a small hill they were surrounded by acres of bright orange poppies and blue morning glories that smothered the air in a honeyed perfume.

The Professor took a deep breath. "Nature reaches out with glorious sights, sounds, and sweet smells, and offers a gentle companionship to anyone willing to embrace it. Our old friend Keats felt its rhythms and rainbows, understood its values, and shared its magic, truth, and beauty through his great odes. He left us such a rich legacy for his twenty-five years. We should all be so generous."

Nudged by a warm breeze, the field of purples and blues began to sway back and forth.

The Professor turned to his companions. "We need to get back here in the fall. We'll pack a lunch and spend part of the day planting acorns. I'll let Herschel and Clementine know when we're coming."

At the parking lot, the Professor shouted at a couple of teenagers after one of them tossed his empty soda can to the ground. The young men responded with a curse, causing Mike to demand he pick up the can and apologize to the Professor. They argued, but complied when Deacon approached.

Deacon, Mike, and the Professor shook hands and agreed to meet the next day.

## What about Bonnie?

On Tuesday, May 20$^{th}$, Deacon, Mike, and the Professor left Saint Louis in Mike's ten-year-old truck for the eight hundred-fifty mile trip to Washington D.C. The Professor sat in the spacious back seat, a couple of suitcases shoved to the side. They had reserved adjacent rooms at the River Inn, a motor lodge off Hwy. 295, thirty miles from the Capitol. The day before they left Deacon learned from Sergeant Craft, the homicide detective checking into Bobby's murder, there were no new leads.

Wednesday afternoon they were on Hwy. 79, not far from Charleston, West Virginia. They planned to get on I-66 and then straight to Washington.

Around two o'clock, they were driving through a wooded region, when Deacon slapped the dashboard. "Pull over and stop."

Mike parked on the side of the road. "OK, now what?"

Deacon got out and walked back toward a small black figure lying on the side of the busy road. A few seconds later, the Professor caught up with him. Mike watched for a moment, and then followed the other two.

Deacon was holding the figure, when Mike caught up, and remarked, "It's only a dead cat."

Deacon examined the tag around the animal's neck. "Her name was Bonnie. I'm calling the number on the tag to let her owners know, they must be frantic." Deacon set the animal down in the grass, and then stepped toward the woods to get away from the noisy traffic.

Mike and the Professor watched Deacon pace back and forth and begin shouting.

Deacon walked up shaking his head. "I talked to some lady, and then a guy. I told them where they could come get their cat, and the jerks didn't seem to care. How do you like that shit!"

Mike shrugged. "I guess we go."

Deacon gestured toward an oak tree about seventy feet from the road. "There's nice grass and good shade under that tree. We'll bury her there. Have you got something we can dig with?"

"There's a small shovel in the back of my truck."

Deacon cradled Bonnie as he and the Professor walked over to the oak tree. She was still soft and warm. The crackling flow of a nearby creek could be heard rounding its way through the woods. To the right of the oak a small stand of blossoming cherry trees shared a warm sweet scent. Pushed by a light breeze, the seventy-degree temperature felt comfortable.

With his sleeves rolled up, Mike approached with a shovel in one hand and a large metal tool box in the other. "I emptied this out, I think she'll fit."

Deacon brushed her eyes close, removed a few specks of gravel from her fur, and then placed her in the tool box.

Mike finished digging, and then reached for the metal box.

Deacon held out his hand. "I want to give her something to take on her journey." He retrieved from his pants pocket a black rosary, kissed the crucifix, and laid the rosary next to the cat. Then he closed the metal box.

Mike placed the box in the hole. Deacon scattered a handful of earth on the box, and then Mike refilled the hole.

After tamping the last of the dirt down with his hands, Mike asked, "Do you want to say a few words?"

Deacon glanced at the traffic shuttling by, and then gazed up at the cloudless sky. "Yes, I do."

The Professor removed his derby, while Mike rolled down his sleeves and dusted off his jeans.

Standing over the small mound of dirt in his white shirt and tan slacks, Deacon made the sign of the cross, and bowed. "Lord, we commend the departing soul of Your good servant—Bonnie. She had a short, tough life, yet I'm sure there were rich moments. Her work is done here, and we know she's been delivered to a better place. I think she will enjoy spending part of her time relaxing in the woods, resting in the shade of an oak tree. You know, cats like their sleep."

Deacon dropped to one knee. "Lord, one more thing. Please introduce Bonnie to another recent arrival, a great guy named Bobby

Aherne. Bobby loves cats, and he and Bonnie will be happy together."

The Professor pointed his cane at a large white stone a few feet away. "Let's use that to mark her grave." Deacon and Mike struggled with the heavy stone, but finally placed it on the small mound of dirt.

When they reached the truck, Deacon noticed a rabbit and two gray squirrels near the grave. Gathered above them on a low hanging branch of the oak tree, a trio of whippoorwills had begun to twitter and sing.

Mike started up the engine. "Deacon, I've seen hundreds of animals in distress or dead. I'm always going to remember this one."

"Death is inevitable, but it doesn't have to be alone, abandoned, and on the side of some damn road. How many so-called nice people drove past her in their cars and trucks? We should be better than that."

## Who is this Mr. Chen?

Mike, Deacon, and the Professor arrived at River Inn lodge a little after ten o'clock, Wednesday evening. After a late supper, they planned to begin their investigation the next day.

They needed to talk to Rebecca Townsend. The cops had interviewed her about the photo, sent anonymously by the Professor, showing Bobby and her in front of Ford's Theater, the evening of his disappearance. Deacon had learned from Sergeant Craft that Ms. Townsend claimed she was just asking directions and didn't know any Bobby Aherne. Following the interview, she vanished. She no longer appeared on Senator's Hodge's website. Professor had called the senator's office, and was told Rebecca Townsend didn't work there. He also gave Mike and Deacon thirty copies of the sketch he had made of the Asian man that delivered the money.

Around seven-thirty Thursday morning, Mike drove Deacon and the Professor a couple miles to Jeannine's, a small café specializing in "country style" dining they passed when they arrived the night before. Built in 1942, the one-story red-brick building seated seventy-five and catered to families, truck drivers, and people pulling off the nearby highway. A gravel lot in back could squeeze parking for forty cars. Founded by Jeannine King, it remained under the same family control. Customers entered through double wooden doors in the back. The cash register was to your right, the scuffed red-oak wood floor was original, and the recessed lighting had been a recent update on the ten-foot ceiling.

Customers seated themselves in either a window booth facing Hwy. 395, or a wooden table with six chairs. That morning several tables had been pushed together to accommodate larger groups.

Mike spotted a booth that had opened up, and the three ran over and sat down. In less than a minute, a young man named Jeff took their order. Mike wanted three sugar-coated jelly donuts and black coffee. Deacon got the breakfast special of bacon and eggs, hash browns, and orange juice.

The Professor studied the menu. "We can't get much work done on an empty stomach." He ordered a big stack of buckwheat pancakes with extra butter, and coffee with cream.

After the server left, the Professor joked. "I love the aroma of bacon on the griddle, coffee fresh brewed, and God's perfect food—fat fluffy pancakes. Throw in cigarette or cigar smoke and you've got a great blend of taste, smell, and atmosphere."

"They've banned that old-school perfection. Tobacco has to stay outside. No sense giving folks cancer with second-hand smoke," Deacon said.

Mike waved the back of his hand. "They came up with second-hand crap to pressure smokers to quit. Science is politicized like everything else these days. And it's nobody's business if I want to risk my health smoking."

The Professor leaned toward Mike. "The law makes us go outside to light up, and that's what counts."

A couple of busboys were arguing over a tip left on a nearby table, when Jeff arrived with the food.

Jeff set a large plate of pancakes in front of the Professor. "My grandmother's recipe—you can't beat them. Top it with oodles of melted butter and maple syrup, and it's the best breakfast you'll ever have."

Deacon asked, "Are these your grandma's eggs?"

"Grandma didn't lay eggs. She did make a great omelet."

"Next time, I'll get an omelet."

Jeff asked if they needed anything else, as he pushed the cart away.

Mike held his donut dripping bright-red jelly. "I'll let you know."

The Professor drenched his pancakes in maple syrup, and said, "We got to get a second vehicle. I called the car rental place across the street, and they've reserved a sedan. When we're done we can run over there and pick it up. It gives us more flexibility to pursue leads."

Deacon glanced over. "At times we'll be split up, which might make us a little more vulnerable to whatever is out there. However, I get your point."

Deacon asked Mike, "Do you want to update Steve and Gary on our progress?"

"Fuckum—they didn't come."

The Professor emptied the rest of the thick syrup onto his plate. "That kid's grandma sure knew her pancakes. These are the best I've ever had.  Have you guys noticed that food loaded with fat always tastes better?"

Deacon winked. "Watch it Professor, fat leads to high cholesterol and heart attacks and strokes.  I'm sure pancakes are next on the banned list."

The Professor dropped his fork on the plate. "Butter, pancakes, plus a cigarette might equal a heart attack.  I'll take my chances."

Mike leaned back in his chair. "One day they'll tell us pancakes create second-hand obesity or high-blood pressures. Nothing is too crazy these days."

They laughed as Jeff refilled their cups.

The Professor tossed the sketch on the table. "Why don't you guys circulate this around town.  Tell folks there's five-thousand bucks for any information about the guy in the sketch. My cell number and first name is on the back.  Money has a way of hoisting people's memories.  And instead of bars and nightclubs, try other venues like trendy restaurants, fitness boutiques, and gift shops. Also, run by Rock Creek Park, where I first saw the guy dropping that cash off.  Bobby checked it out, but who knows, a jogger might remember him this time.  I'll search for Rebecca Townsend, the young gal that set Bobby up.  Her parents got a lot of bucks and live in Manhattan.  And Deacon,  give Sergeant Craft a call.  Pretend you're in St. Louis, and checking the status of the investigation. He might share a piece of information we can use."

The Professor pulled out his gold pocket watch.

"That is a beautiful timepiece," Mike said.

"I bought it twenty years ago while vacationing in Greece.  My wife and I were in Athens strolling down a side street and saw it displayed in a pawn shop.  The proprietor of the shop told us an elderly woman dressed in black had brought it in several years before, and never returned.  A few minutes later, I walked out with it in my vest pocket. The watch is a hundred years old and keeps perfect time."

"I wonder who that old lady was, and why she pawned such a nice watch."

"My wife wondered who created the watch and how many other hands it might have passed through before it got to me. Like that Grecian Urn, I'll bet it's lived an interesting life."

The Professor shoved the watch in his vest pocket. "It's nine o'clock. Let's see what we can shake loose."

# R.I.P. When All is Said and Done

Mike and Deacon dropped the Professor off at the car rental place, and then drove to Rock Creek Park. There they headed in opposite directions, each with a handful of sketches.

Mike covered Valley Trail, a five-and-a-half-mile nature trail that snaked through the park, and where the Professor saw the exchange. He talked with a number of joggers, bikers, and even a couple of horseback riders. He got a few maybes, but nothing he could use.

Deacon canvased the picnic area. He ran into a lot of out-of-town families, none recognized the man in the sketch. He stopped to eat barbequed chicken wings and listen to bluegrass music with a family from a small town in Georgia. Their grandfather was killed during WWII, and they planned to visit the World War II Memorial.

Around twelve-thirty, Mike was waiting at the truck when Deacon arrived carrying a brown grocery bag.

Mike asked, "What do you have there?"

Deacon set the bag inside the truck. "It's your lunch compliments of Grandma Kirby. There are half-dozen barbequed chicken wings wrapped in silver paper, and a plate with potato salad, coleslaw, four deviled eggs, and two cans of root beer. She even threw in a bunch of chocolate chip cookies. What more could a guy want."

Mike scrounged through the bag. "Who the hell is Grandma Kirby?"

"She's the matriarch of a family I ran into from Georgia. I showed them the sketch, and the next thing they invite me to sit with them and eat. I spent an hour talking and listening to music. It felt like a picnic in our neighborhood's good old days. When I told them I had a buddy waiting for me that sweet old lady grabbed me by the arm. A couple minutes later she hands me this bundle of goodies and said it's for your friend."

Mike raised a chicken wing in the air. "Let's hear it for sweet old ladies everywhere."

"They were good folks."

Mike tossed Deacon one of the cans of root beer, and then grabbed a deviled egg. Fifteen minutes later, they shoved the empty bag and plate into a nearby waste can

On the way back to the truck, Mike said, "This is like searching for a needle in a haystack. A couple of folks wanted to know why I was asking about the guy. I claimed he was witness to something, and then threw in the five-thousand dollar reward."

They agreed the park was a waste of time, and decided to spend the rest of the afternoon and next few days checking out gyms and fitness clubs.

Deacon spotted a park ranger. "Maybe he's seen our man."

"It won't hurt to ask." Mike ran over and showed him the sketch.

The ranger glanced at the picture. "I haven't seen this guy for a few weeks. He seemed a little strange, but wasn't breaking any rules or causing any problems. What do you want him for?"

"He witnessed an accident, and an insurance company is paying us to find him and get a statement."

Deacon mentioned the potential of five-thousand dollars.

The ranger stared at the sketch, and then signaled another ranger. "Hey, Greg, remember this guy?"

"Sure, that's Mr. Chen. I haven't seen him in a while. What's up?"

"These guys claim he's an important witness to something. There could be five grand in it if we help find him."

Greg grabbed the sketch. "I can tell you he likes to work out, and is into karate. You ought to check into some of the gyms and martial art clubs around town."

Mike thanked them. "Keep the sketch, and call the number on the back if you see the guy or come up with anything else." He got their phone numbers and promised to call if the lead panned out.

Mike glanced at Deacon, as they drove off. "We got a last name; know he's into martial arts, and where he might hang out. Not bad for a few hours work."

Deacon rolled down the window. "Let's do some research."

Around seven-thirty, Thursday evening, Mike, Deacon, and the Professor were sharing notes and planning next moves at the Professor's motel room. After leaving the park, Mike and Deacon had spent the rest of the afternoon developing a list they would contact in the greater Washington, D.C. area. They came up with twenty names, addresses, and phone numbers.

Mike showed the list to the Professor. "Plans are to call these places tomorrow and ask if Mr. Chen has arrived. If we get a positive hit, we head over there. Anyway, that's our Friday."

The Professor scanned the list. "Call me if you run into this Mr. Chen. Take a picture and send it to me, and I'll let you know if it's the guy I saw in the park."

The Professor opened the refrigerator. "I picked up a twelve-pack of beer, and there's a bottle of Scotch on the counter."

Mike grabbed a beer, while Deacon poured the Scotch, adding ice and water for himself and the Professor.

The Professor sipped his Scotch. "I spent most of the day online. Rebecca Townsend's parents live in Manhattan. I discovered they have a second home in Georgetown, plus a vacation cabin in the Catskills. The Georgetown address is about a twenty minute drive from here. I'll start there. Call if you think you found our man—Mr. Chen. Assuming that's his real name.

"Oh, I saw on television where Senator Hodge was heading to Iowa next week. She's leading her party in all the polls for President. She's even ahead of our current President. I wonder if whatever we find might screw up her plans."

Mike said, "I'm not from Oregon, yet know enough to know I don't like her. Like a lot of folks in Washington, she's fucking arrogant. I'm sick of that shit."

The Professor agreed. "Me and Bobby saw her with Attorney General Kidd at Barnacle's. They greeted everyone, and then headed to a room in the back. Ah, to be a fly on that room's wall."

Mike tossed his empty. "Driving back we passed Gilly's sports bar. Let's do our thinking and drinking there. It's a few blocks, we can walk. The Cardinals are playing the Nationals."

## R.I.P. When All is Said and Done

Friday morning, the Professor headed to Georgetown and the Townsend address on Cathedral Ave. NW, near the intersection of Massachusetts and Wisconsin Avenues.

A little after ten o'clock, the Professor spotted the address on the tree-lined street paved with gray worn cobble stones. He parked around the corner next to Cato's, a small jewelry store. After glancing at several gold pocket watches on display in the window, he headed back up to Cathedral Avenue.

The Townsend's three-story home showcased a third-floor balcony with a decorative black railing surrounded by lush green ivy clinging to the red-brick facade. A four-foot high cast-iron fence surrounded the property. There was a Koi pond to the right of the metal entrance gate, and a dozen trimmed red and yellow rose plants lining the steps leading to a large gray wooden porch with twin ten-foot dark stained oak front entrance doors. Three tall red maples extended shade over most of the front yard and sidewalk. A late-model dark-blue Mercedes was parked on the street in front of the house. Homes in this neighborhood listed from four to six million dollars, and up.

The Professor strolled past the residence tapping his cane against the sidewalk. He then opened the metal gate, glanced at the Koi pond, and went to the front door. After several rings and knocks, he decided he could wait and watch from the patio at Cassy's Café, down the block.

Cassy's advertised itself as "Elite Eating." It attracted preppy college students, young professionals, rich old-guard, and power diners including presidents, senators, and moneyed globalists. Its menu included grilled crab cakes, filet mignon, strawberries jubilee, red pepper-salmon pasta, and one of the best wine cellars in the city.

The Professor settled in with his coffee and lemon sweet roll, and studied the crowded patio. He counted lots of wagging fingers and righteous sneers. At the next table, a twenty-something ordered an espresso, and dropped a hundred dollar tip. Young and old pointed and poked while yelling, "Fuck this, and fuck that." Metal chairs scraped and clawed the concrete as hurried elites came and went. And there was lots of wisecracking about places and folks out there in that other world—the wasteland. The conversations and looks were cold with a touch of practiced and permanent contempt. He thought of tossing his hot coffee at someone, but couldn't pick a favorite target.

Half way through his sweet roll, the Professor noticed a young man in dusty brown work clothes watering the roses at the Townsend home. He finished his coffee, left a five-dollar tip, and headed back.

A couple minutes later, the Professor stood in front of the house tapping his cane against the metal fence, and then he opened the gate.

The young man dropped the hose, and faced the Professor. "Can I help you?"

The Professor removed his derby. "Yes, is Rebecca Townsend at home? I'd like to talk to her about a mutual acquaintance."

"She's not here. I don't know when she might be available."

"Can I leave my card?"

"Yes, sir."

The Professor scribbled, *a friend of Bobby*, on the back of the card, and handed it to the young man.

He shoved the card in his pocket. "I'll see she gets it."

The Professor noticed movement behind curtains in a third-floor window to the right of the balcony. He couldn't tell if it was man or woman, but knew he was being watched as he headed to his car.

Friday evening, after dinner, they met in the Professor's motel room to review and plan the weekend.

The Professor poured the Scotch, and handed Mike a can of cold beer. "At lunch I sampled Washington's "wise guys" at Cassy's Cafe. Even with a mouth full of food or booze, they can't stop criticizing, moralizing, and pretending they're better than everyone else."

The Professor took a drink. "Anyway, I'm sure I tapped a nerve at the Townsend home. Somebody was watching me from the third-floor window. It could have been Rebecca. I left a business card. Let's see if I get a call."

Deacon said, "We moved the needle. Found a gym where the manager recognized the sketch and confirmed the man's name as Chen. We also got a first name—Joe. The guy used to work out there a least twice a week, but hasn't been seen in over a month. Even waving the five-thousand, I couldn't budge an address or phone number from the manager. Nothing came up in an Internet search. Maybe this Joe Chen is in hiding or left the country."

The Professor said, "We'll post the sketch with the name Joe Chen on social media sites with the five-thousand dollar offer for information on his current whereabouts. Let's see if a little more publicity generates moves from Chen or others. Of course, going public puts our names out there. Somebody plays rough."

Mike leaned back in his chair. "Don't worry about us."

The Professor added. "My gut tells me Rebecca is a bit player in all this. She can't be more than twenty or twenty one."

Deacon asked, "What about Senator Hodge?"

"I don't know if Hodge had anything to do with Bobby's death. Let's build a fire under Chen and Rebecca and see where it goes."

"How much do we share with Sergeant Craft?"

Mike raised his hands in the air. "Why share anything with those guys?"

The Professor finished his drink. "Let's see what we come up with and then decide who to bring in."

Mike and Deacon spent several days peppering Internet sites around the world with Joe Chen posters offering a cool five-thousand for information on his whereabouts. Payable when contact with him was made. They included their cellphone and email addresses.

The Professor continued to stroll past the Townsend home waving at upper floor windows and tapping his cane on the sidewalk. Stopping now and then for a coffee and sweet roll at Cassy's.

Within a few hours of their first postings, Mike and Deacon were getting calls and emails about Joe Chen from around the world. A few kidding, some serious, but none leading anywhere. One from Hong Kong and another from Singapore offered the most promise.

The first break came on Wednesday, the second week they were in Washington, around two in the afternoon. The Professor was relaxing at Cassy's with a coffee and glazed donut, when his cellphone rang. The caller's number read "private."

"This is Professor Mason."

After a moment of silence, the caller responded. "I'm Rebecca Townsend. Professor Mason, I understand you're a friend of Bobby, the fellow murdered a while back."

"We were partners investigating—maybe high-level corruption. And you were the last person I saw him with the night he disappeared. You lied to the cops about your encounter with him. I watched from the other side of the street."

"I didn't kill Bobby, and didn't know he got murdered until I heard about it on the news the next day. I'm sick of what they did to him, and scared of the people behind it."

"Do you want to do something about this?"

"Yes."

"Then we'll meet, and you fill me in on what you know."

"We have to be careful. A couple of guys told my gardener that I shouldn't talk to the cops, or anyone else."

"Is there a place we can get together?"

"Let me think about it, and I'll call you later today. OK?"

"That will work."

The Professor phoned Deacon. "Rebecca Townsend has agreed to meet. She's supposed to call me back with the where and when."

Deacon put his phone on speaker so Mike could listen, and then said, "Bobby ended up dead the last time she agreed to meet. Do we trust her?"

"That's the rub. She claims she didn't kill Bobby, and feels bad about him. She says she's scared, and wants to help. I think we meet, as long as it's not an abandoned warehouse near the river."

Mike jumped into the conversation. "It has to be a place we can keep sight of you."

"She said she's being watched, so we need to keep our eyes open for others."

"Watched by whom—the cops?"

"Not the cops. Watched by people behind all this, whoever the hell that is."

Deacon reminded the Professor. "Ask her about Joe Chen? We've gotten a few interesting calls and emails from a guy over in Singapore. Yet nothing we can use so far."

"Find out who killed Bobby, or if she can point us in the right direction. That's why we're here," Mike said.

"I'll call as soon as I hear from her, and then we develop a plan. Talk to you guys later."

Friday morning, the Professor got his call from Rebecca Townsend. She proposed they meet that evening at eight o'clock at the Grand Bijou, an old movie theater on 11${}^{th}$ St. NW.

Rebecca stammered. "Professor Mason, I've watched you prance back and forth in front of my parent's house wearing that black derby and lavender bow tie."

"You like it?"

"Wear something different tonight. The people watching me must have noticed you strolling past my house. Get into something like a sweatshirt, jeans, and maybe tennis shoes. Please lose that hat, and shave that crazy mustache. Also, is it possible to get by without that cane?"

"I'll pick up some clothes this morning, and shave back the mustache. Not having the cane will slow me up a little, but I'll get by."

"OK, you won't have trouble finding the place. It's a two-story brick building with a marquee that lights the block. On the weekends the Bijou runs old-time movies starring folks like Bogart, Cooper, and Clark Gable. This weekend is devoted to Veronica Lake movies, and they'll run them from six-thirty tonight to ten o'clock Sunday night. Women who come dressed like Veronica Lake get in for half-price, so the place will be filled with ladies who look pretty much the same. I'll leave in street clothes, but stuffed in a paper bag have a big blond wig and a dress like Lake wore in *The Blue Dahlia*. I'll change in the theater bathroom and come out appearing like hundreds of others. I'll lose any folks following me in the crowd."

"How will I find you?"

"Don't worry, I'll spot you. Hang out near the cigarette machines, and wear a Cardinal baseball cap. I'll contact you there, and we'll head off to the balcony area and get the privacy we need."

"Be careful, and I'll see you around eight o'clock."

The Professor filled his partners in on the plan. Mike and Deacon decided to arrive at the theater around seven o'clock and stake out the cigarette and candy area. From there they could check for signs of a set-up. The Professor would drive himself, and get there about seven-thirty.

## Breakthrough at the Grand Bijou

Mike parked a few blocks away on a side street, and then he and Deacon hiked it over to the theater. Built in 1922, the Grand Bijou's massive two-story faded-brown brick building took up a third of the block. It had seen better times, yet retained most of its character and charm. Its one-screen seated fifteen hundred, including five hundred in the balcony. Hollywood's biggest and brightest stars had stood out front as movies often premiered here in the 1930s and '40s.

It had been over sixty years since a movie opened here, but tonight had the feel of a long-ago gala premiere. Limousines and cabs dropped off women in 1940s style dress and long blond hair. Laughing, smiling, snapping pictures, they strolled under the Grand Bijou's large marquee as it beamed bright gold—VERONICA LAKE.

You entered through one of six glass doors. Your feet sunk a half inch as you walked on the thick cushy light-tan lobby carpet. The white lobby walls held dozens of colorful yesteryear movie posters starring Veronica Lake.

A few minutes past seven o'clock, Mike bought a pack of cigarettes and a couple of candy bars while Deacon eyeballed for anything suspicious. The large busy lobby was packed with Lake Pretenders of all sizes: tall, small, heavy, young and old. One thing they had in common, the long, flowing blond hair—the Lake Look. Some wore wigs, while others had dyed their hair. Lines at the concession stand were long, slow moving, and selling lots of chocolate bars, super-sized sodas, and popcorn that filled the air with that buttery theater smell. Folks were still pouring in while the movie *This Gun for Hire* played.

Mike handed Deacon a chocolate bar. "I glanced at the movie, and saw this gorgeous young, thin gal. Draped over her right eye she had this long blond hair—very sexy. Her voice purred. That must have been Veronica Lake."

"Yes and there's been nothing like her since. All the women wanted to copy her blond peek-a-boo style, and men wanted to be with her. That beautiful lady sat on top of the world, and by the time she was thirty the stardom was over. She died tragically at fifty, but left us a lot of great films."

Mike glimpsed over Deacon's shoulder. "The Professor is here. I'll head to the other side of the room."

Seventy-two and pudgy, the Professor leaned against the wall near the cigarette machines wearing dark-blue slacks, white tennis shoes, gray sweatshirt, and red baseball cap. Deacon and Mike watched from opposite sides of the busy concession area.

At eight o'clock, a tall blonde in a beige dress that fell an inch below the knees walked up to the Professor, and whispered, "I'm Rebecca Townsend."

The Professor nodded. "It's nice to finally meet you."

She grabbed him by the arm. "Follow me. There's a place in the second-floor balcony where we can have privacy."

Mike and Deacon watched the Professor slowly ascend the bold-red carpeted stairs, led by an attentive blonde.

"Whew, she could give Veronica Lake a run for her money. What a babe. I hope she didn't have anything to do with killing Bobby," Mike said.

The Professor gripped the thick cherry-stained mahogany railing as he worked his way up the twenty-one stairs leading to the balcony. Rebecca pointed to a darkened area of empty seats at the end of the top row.

Mike and Deacon, staying about thirty feet back, trailed the Professor up the stairs, and then took separate balcony seats a few rows away from the Professor. Too far to listen in on the conversation, yet close enough to act if needed.

Rebecca leaned toward the Professor; brushing the long blond hairs away from her blue eyes. "They followed me here. I ducked into the restroom and walked out with five other blondes, and melted into the crowd. They must be still hanging around."

The Professor removed his Cardinal cap. "Followed by whom?"

"I'm sure they work for the Clearing House, the organization behind all of this."

"What or who is the Clearing House?"

"Its headquartered in a twenty-story building near the Changi Airport in Singapore. I've never been there. The Singapore Man told me they got the whole building to themselves."

"What do they do, and how does it involve me and you?"

"Those guys act as middle-man for anything and everything. I've picked up payments for Senator Hodge a half-dozen times. I'd drop off money from Senator Hodge if she needed to buy something. Judges sell decisions, legislators write laws in a certain way or find a reason not to write them at all. Even scientists fake results if the price is right. It seems anything can be purchased, or bartered, or traded for something. They take ten percent of the value of a deal, and charge it to the persons or groups doing the deal."

"How do you know this?"

"I learned a lot of details from the Singapore Man. Senator Hodge also clued me in on a lot of stuff. My mom and the senator went to school together, and my parents contribute to her campaigns. That's how I got the intern job. I was there less than a month when the senator started having me make those pickups in the park. They weren't always cash. It could be precious jewelry, expensive coins, stamps, even valuable paintings in exchange for an accommodation. Everybody acted so casual about it. I figured that's the way the world works in Washington and everywhere. I got five-hundred dollars every time, and it didn't seem like anybody was getting hurt—until that fellow Bobby got killed."

"Do you have any physical records, recordings, pictures, on any of this?"

"I have my word, plus time and dates when exchanges were made. I can't even guess what deals were being bought and paid for. I never asked. The Singapore Man must know."

"Is he this Joe Chen character? The guy I saw dropping money off in the park a few months back."

"Yeah, his name is Joe Chen. I've always called him the Singapore Man. He told me he has physical records and evidence from over the years. He called it his 'just in case' stash."

"What did he mean by that?"

"A way of protecting himself in case something goes wrong. He bragged he has the goods on a lot of people."

A woman screamed below the balcony. The theater lights came on as Rebecca peeked over the railing. Two Asian men were dragging a woman toward the exit sign. Within a few seconds they were surrounded by theater security and a couple of police officers. The young woman's blond wig lay on the floor and her face was bloody and bruised. After some kicking and punches, the men, under a hail of popcorn, candy bars and plastic soda cups, got hauled out in handcuffs.

Mike elbowed Deacon, as they watched the commotion. "We could take those two punks."

Deacon nodded. "Let's hope there aren't any others around."

While the police interviewed witnesses the woman was carried to a waiting ambulance. After an additional twenty-minute delay, the lights in the theater dimmed and the movie resumed.

Rebecca scrunched down in her seat. ""My God, that could have been me! Those are the guys who followed me here."

The Professor put his hand on Rebecca's shoulder. "Folks jump into things and before they know it everything is out of control. We can help each other."

Rebecca grabbed the Professor's hand. "All I wanted to do was make a few extra bucks while finishing my degree, and gather a few networking contacts while in Washington. Everybody does that. I'm a nice person. After that guy Bobby got killed my parents told me to hide out for a while and avoid further contact with the cops. Yet the problem never seemed to go away. Now it's gotten even worse. Professor Mason, what do you want me to do? I can't hide out forever."

"Tell the truth to the authorities when the time comes. Mr. Joe Chen sounds like the person who could bust this wide open. If he's got details, data, documents—the proof. We need him and his information in the hands of law enforcement and journalists out there. Jam it in front of the public before that so-called Clearing House manages to cover-up the truth or kill everyone they think is a threat to all this. Could you talk him into helping us?"

## R.I.P. When All is Said and Done

"He's in hiding. He told me an old friend from the Clearing House came by his apartment and tried to kill him. Joe's on the move and mad. He'll talk to the right people."

"Why do his people want him dead?"

"He said it started with Bobby's death. Killing Bobby didn't bother them. The fact Bobby's murder was mentioned in the news, and then the police got called in. That bothered them. Now somebody is posting a sketch of Joe all over the Internet, asking questions about his whereabouts. They even list Joe's last name. The Clearing House doesn't like all this publicity and figure Joe is a loose end they need to close. They must figure I'm a loose end, too."

"Why doesn't he run to the cops or a media outlet and tell all he knows? Blow the thing up that way?"

"He doesn't know who to trust. Over the years he or others have worked with almost everyone in Washington. Name the town: New York, London, Tokyo, Shanghai, Rome, even Moscow. The Clearing House has its fingers everywhere. He figured if he went to a major media outlet, they would bury the story and contact the Clearing House, and then he disappears. He thought about spreading what he knows on social media, but no one takes their stuff seriously. Plus, the Clearing House has the power to take anything he posts down."

"Where is he now?"

"He knows they're watching the airports and bus stations, so he's living out of his car, moving around here in Washington. He's been using cash and switched to a burner phone."

"Did Joe or one of his friends kill Bobby?"

"I don't know who killed Bobby, or why. I'll bet Joe knows."

The Professor stretched in the blue cushioned seat. "Give him my number the next time he calls. You'll have to convince him to trust me. That should be easy. It's either me or waiting for the gang at the Clearing House to catch up with him."

"You'll get a call."

Gunshots and screams rang out, causing Rebecca to duck below the seat.

The Professor glanced at the movie screen. "Don't worry. This movie ends in a blaze of gunfire. Somebody always eats a bullet in a Veronica Lake movie. That's Hollywood in the Thirties and Forties. I don't know if due process was better then, but it got done in less than two hours."

The theater lights came on as *This Gun for Hire* ended. While the credits rolled, a loudspeaker announced a fifteen-minute intermission, and then *The Glass Key* would start at nine o'clock.

The Professor asked, "Where will you go?"

"I won't let my parents get caught in the cross-hairs of my problems. I can't go back to their Georgetown home, or their places in Manhattan or the Catskills. Get this, a couple days ago I called Senator Hodge to complain I was being watched, and she didn't take my call. I left a message, and she hasn't called back. I guess she's got a campaign to run, and I've become one of those throw-away loose ends. What a phony jerk—don't vote for her."

Rebecca thought a moment. "I'll leave my car where I parked it and grab a cab. I have a couple of sorority girlfriends whose parents have places here in town. I'm sure one of them will put me up for a while."

"OK—good. I'll wait for Mr. Chen's call. Also, phone me every day at six in the evening—no matter what. That way I'll know you're safe, and you can update me with anything new. You ought to start using a burner phone."

Rebecca adjusted her long blond wig, reached over and hugged the Professor, and then left.

After she was out of sight, Mike and Deacon sat next to the Professor.

The Professor stretched his legs and shared what Rebecca had told him.

Mike asked, "Do we believe her?"

"I think she's too scared to lie."

"OK, let's see what this Chen has to say. Meanwhile, I'm getting a big tub of hot-buttered popcorn and a supersized cola. *The Glass Key* starts in ten minutes."

"That sounds good," Deacon said.

The Professor sat back down. "Grab me a couple of chocolate bars while you're up there. And make sure they're dark chocolate."

Tired and groggy, they left at six the next morning after the conclusion of *I Married a Witch*.

## Handle Justice with Care

Mike, Deacon, and the Professor got together a little past three o'clock, Saturday afternoon for a late lunch of pizza, sodas, and Mike with his fries and chocolate shake.

Mike smeared a handful of fries in ketchup. "Those black and white movies are fun, and Veronica Lake was gorgeous. I got to watch more of them."

Deacon nodded. "She was great in *The Glass Key*. I've seen it before, and I still love the surprise ending."

The Professor leaned back. "I enjoy watching those great old movie stars running around the screen laughing, fighting, kissing, and confronting problems large and small. It's easy to get lost for a couple of hours. But when the credits roll I'm reminded everyone in that movie is long dead, and their big houses and swimming pools now belong to someone else."

Mike glanced over. "Come on, Professor, we're all on the clock. The only rule is when you're kicked, always kick back. No point sweating anything else."

Deacon set his glass down. "Let's enjoy her movies and leave it there."

Mike changed the subject to soccer, and then they ordered coffee and discussed politics.

Joe Chen called a little after five o'clock. He sounded nervous and in a hurry to get together. He and the Professor decided to meet at seven thirty that evening at Killard's, an all-night service station a few miles from Arlington Cemetery. So Joe could recognize him, the Professor agreed to wear his Cardinal baseball cap, and lavender bowtie.

After he hung up, the Professor said to Mike, "I'll drive over there and meet this guy, while you boys take the truck. Rebecca has convinced him I'm their best way out. They don't know about you guys. Get there ahead of me. I don't want to spook him with the three of us showing up at once."

"This could be a set-up."

"It's possible, but I don't think so. Chen told me he abandoned his car a few days ago and moves around in taxis."

"You can't have a meeting at a service station. And we have to control where you guys end up. Got a place in mind?"

"Over in Ashton Heights, there's a Catholic grade school that closed a few years ago. I drove by a couple of days ago, and the place is empty, even a few broken windows. They called it Saint Catherine's, and it's near the intersection of North Person and Washington Blvd. We can slip into the gymnasium. I'll give you guys a call when we head over there."

After buying a couple of battery operated lanterns, Mike and Deacon arrived at Killard's around seven-fifteen. Mike reached under the seat and offered Deacon a .38 caliber pistol.

Deacon stared at the weapon. "I don't think we need it."

Mike shoved it inside his belt. "We know this guy runs with a rough crowd, and he might have something to do with Bobby's death."

Deacon surveyed the station lot while Mike gassed up the truck. A few minutes later, they walked inside and bought a couple bags of chips. While they were talking with the clerk, a cab rolled up and a thin, dark haired man of Asian descent got out. Wearing gray slacks, and light-blue windbreaker, he appeared to be in his thirties.

Mike elbowed Deacon. "There's our guy."

The man paid the cabbie, and then stood near the door. He glanced around the station lot while keeping his right hand inside his jacket pocket.

Mike pulled Deacon aside. "He's packing."

At that moment the Professor, wearing his red baseball cap, pulled up in his sedan with the driver's side window rolled down. He spotted Chen and waved him over to his car.

Mike started out the door, when Deacon grabbed his arm. "I don't think he wants trouble. If the Professor wins his confidence, we know where he's going to drive the guy."

Chen and the Professor talked for a few minutes through the open window, and then Chen got in the car and they shook hands. The Professor pulled out of the parking lot. Mike and Deacon followed at a discrete distance.

The Professor offered his passenger a cigarette, and the conversation began to flow. The next hour they drove around Washington, passing Ford's Theatre and then the Washington Monument.

The Professor checked the rear-view mirror, and then glanced at Joe. "How did you get so far from home?"

"Work brought me to your country, and many other countries."

"What kind of work?"

"I talked it over with Rebecca, so I think you know."

"I know in very general terms: corruption, payoffs, vote buying, and sometimes murder. Rebecca told me you have details, and that's what we need."

"You mentioned we—who is we?"

"There's me, a police officer here in Washington named Bill Craft, and a couple of friends of mine. And, of course Rebecca agreed to help us against an organization called the Clearing House."

Joe flipped his cigarette out the window. "Yeah, she said they tried to grab her at the theater the other night."

Joe glanced at a white limousine that sped past on the right. "It's just the five of you? That ain't much considering what you're up against. They got power everywhere, from people in high places to guys on the streets with guns. The Clearing House has been around for a hundred years. It moves things and makes the world work the way it does. They were globalists before the term got popular. They helped both sides during World War II."

The Professor pulled over while a black Jeep sped by with two police cars, red lights flashing, in pursuit.

The Professor watched the flashing lights disappear, and then asked, "Now tell me about the Clearing House. How did you get with those folks?"

"I grew up in a section of Singapore called Little India, and got recruited right off the streets at the age of sixteen. They have a formal training program where they teach you how to do things their way. They got a whole trade school devoted to future leaders of their organization. Now and then, they contract out for hits and other things. However, you have to be born in Singapore to be made a formal member—no outsiders. I gave them twenty years of my life, and now they want me dead. And they don't give pardons or last minute reprieves."

"Why do they want you dead?"

"A few months back I made a drop at Rock Creek Park. A Russian oligarch bought Senator Hodge's vote on a piece of trade legislation. A standard cash deal, a cool half million. The problem was someone spotted me and Rebecca making the exchange. Next thing I know, Rebecca told me someone was floating a picture of her holding the cash, and asking a lot of questions. Things like that concern the folks at the Clearing House."

"What happened then?"

"Then this guy Bobby shows up at Rebecca's apartment. He claims he knows all kinds of things. We weren't sure what to make of it. What did he see? Did he know anything? We knew he didn't go to the cops or FBI, because the Clearing House has sources at both places. Anyway, he hands Rebecca a picture of her holding cash, and on the back was written, 'We know what's going on. The word 'We' stood out. I was ordered to find out what he knew, and if anyone else was involved."

The Professor pulled up to stoplight, and glanced over at Joe. "It sounds simple enough. So how does this guy Bobby end up dead?"

Joe folded his hands. "He got shot by accident."

"How does someone get kidnapped, beat up, and then shot by accident? They're already investigating this, so if we go to the cops, they'll want to know those details."

"Rebecca gets him to head down this alley, where four of us were waiting. The son-of-bitch was strong as hell. I hit him with a knockout drug, and we got him in the back seat of the car. We told Rebecca we wanted to talk to the guy and bribe information from him. I showed her the hundred-thousand dollars I brought, and that was the plan."

Joe asked for another cigarette. "We take him to a 'safe house' near the Foggy Bottom area of the city. The guy is propped in a chair with his arms tied. I offer him the hundred thousand. Instead of accepting it he gets mad and mean. He spits at me. Money won't work, so we get a little rough. That doesn't work either, this guy won't budge. I couldn't tell my people I didn't get the information, so I decided to wave my gun at him in a threatening manner. Make him think I would shoot him if he didn't talk."

Joe gazed out the window. "I'm standing close waving the gun and he kicks me and the gun goes off. I didn't want him dead, yet there he was. I never shot anyone before, I get paid to drop off or pick up stuff. All he had to do was tell us what we wanted to know, he gets his money, and everybody goes home."

The Professor tightened his grip on the steering wheel, and said, "Really?"

Joe hesitated for a second, and then continued. "Anyway, we dumped the body under a bridge and took off. The next day the cops and the media got involved. The guy's death didn't bother the folks at the Clearing House. What they won't tolerate are clumsy mistakes and unnecessary publicity. Plus they still didn't know what he knew or whether he was tied to anyone else. Then someone started floating a sketch of me with my name on social media, offering a reward for my whereabouts."

Joe shook his head. "A few days ago, out of the blue my best friend shows up at my apartment. I've known this guy my whole life. I'm heading to the kitchen to get us a drink, and he pulls a gun. I wrestled it away and knocked him out. I've been on the run ever since."

The Professor spun onto Washington Ave. "What are your plans? Run to the cops and confess, and hope the folks at the Clearing House don't catch up with you?"

"Nope, I'm going to deal my way out of all this. The problem is I don't know who to reach out to. There's so much corruption, and the folks at the Clearing House have influence everywhere."

"Well, Joe, you can count on my friends—including Rebecca. What do you have to deal?"

"I've got the names of judges, senators, governors, corporate leaders, and even a former vice president of the U.S. and his son who have sold and bought things through the Clearing House."

"They're going to need more than your word. Where's your proof of all this?"

"I've collected twenty years' worth of evidence. It includes logs of times, dates, places, of what got bought and sold, and with whom. In recent years, I've been taking pictures of some of the players. I got an envelope handed to me by a well-known senator with her fingerprints on it. I've got documents detailing off-shore bank accounts used by big shots to hide or launder money. Besides

America, people all across Europe and the Far East are involved. The Clearing House activities have always been global. I even have a list of so-called suicides and disappearances I know were contract hits."

"A good investigator could bring down a lot if they had access to your data. Assuming they were honest."

"I've got plenty of evidence tucked away in a safe place. It's honesty that's hard to come by. That's why the Clearing House is doing so well. I need a person I can trust—in a hurry."

"You can trust me and my friends—including Rebecca. We're all committed to seeing justice done. I can take you to them tonight, or drop you back at the service station and let your gangster friends eventually catch up with you. Which do you prefer?"

"Let's get something to eat—I'm starving. Then we can meet your friends."

The Professor called Deacon. "We're going to grab some fast food. I'll see you at Saint Catherine's in a half hour."

Saint Catherine's had been a thriving high school, with five-hundred articulate, committed students and clergy of the Catholic faith. The number had shrunk to sixty-eight when it closed a couple of years earlier. The singing, learning, and spiritual commitments now replaced with overgrown grass and weeds, broken windows, and a few noisy, inarticulate rodents. Mike parked in the back, then he and Deacon grabbed the lanterns from the bed of the truck.

After they forced open the gym door, Mike quipped, "Well, Deacon, another church on the trash heap. Give it five fucking years and it will be St. Pius. What do you think God makes of all this?"

"I don't have the answer."

"Let me know when you've figured it out."

"You'll be the first."

Deacon found metal folding chairs lying near the old bleachers. The wooden gym floor had layers of crust and dirt.

Mike held his nose. "Damn it stinks like a pack of old baloney left lying in the sun all day. Probably some animal crawled off and died in here. I'll break a few windows to let in more air."

The lanterns created enough light to conduct a quiet meeting, though not too much to draw attention from the outside.

Mike shoved his .38 pistol in his waistband. "When he walks through the door, I'm disarming that Joe character. This whole thing will work a lot better if we got all the guns."

The Professor parked next to Mike's truck, and reached for his cane.

Joe grabbed the Professor's arm. "I don't need this." After handing over his gun, Joe took the bags loaded with hamburgers, drinks, and fries, and followed the Professor toward the dim light in the gym.

Deacon had set four metal folding chairs in the center of the room. Joe's chair faced the other three chairs lined side by side, with about five feet separating them from him. Mike put Joe's gun near the bleachers, and then they dug into the bags of fast food.

The Professor said, "Joe has a big story to tell, and it comes with the kind of hard evidence even this town can't ignore. We need to listen before deciding what to do."

Joe slung his windbreaker over the back of his chair, and glanced at the Professor. "Where's Rebecca?"

"After we sort things out, we'll call her. Then we meet up with a Sergeant Bill Craft, on the D.C. police force. He'll drive it from there. If there's enough evidence, the FBI will want to get involved. Maybe even the CIA."

They spent fifteen minutes in the semi-dark eating. Deacon lamented the loss of another house of worship, and worried too many things were headed in the wrong direction. The Professor agreed. Joe mentioned a wife and small son back in Singapore. Mike strolled around the old gym and asked the others if they thought any sinners, lost souls, or saints might still be hanging around—maybe to provide guidance.

The Professor set his half-empty soda cup next to his chair, and then walked over and rested his hand on Joe's shoulder.

Joe's jet-black hair was short in the back and nothing flowing over his ears. He was about five-foot four and thin boned. A couple days' worth of beard covered his pock-marked face. A gold upper tooth glistened in the dim light as his large dark eyes scanned the room. While reaching into the bag for another hamburger, he glanced at Mike with a half-smile. Mike noticed a tattoo of a tiger on Joe's right forearm.

A strong breeze pushed through the broken windows. It smelled and felt like rain was on the way. One of the lanterns began to flicker.

The Professor asked Joe, "Why don't you share what you know about the gang from Singapore, and what those folks have been up to?"

Joe leaned toward Mike and Deacon. "How much do you guys know about an organization called the Clearing House?"

Deacon answered. "A little bit, just what the Professor learned from Rebecca. Everything we've heard is bad."

Joe spent twenty minutes sharing much of what he had told the Professor, adding details about bribing a Supreme Court Justice, several Ambassadors, and a Washington five-star hotel bought a couple months ago by the Clearing House.

Deacon asked, "How come I've never heard of this organization?"

"They're subtle and slick, and got dirt on everybody—so no one talks. They eliminate anyone considered a threat. I got careless with that payment to the senator and now they're after me."

The Professor interrupted. "You were unlucky—not careless. I happened to be resting in the grass nearby. A million to one thing, and here we are."

"I've always had bad luck. I've moved diamonds, valuable paintings, and historical documents. A few years back I got a job as a server at Cassy's Café, and dropped a packet of emeralds in the coffee I served to the vice president of the U.S. That son-of-a-bitch and his son had to be the greediest bastards in Washington, and they had a lot of competition. He had his hand out every week. This one old senator who would sell his vote if I provided a red-headed prostitute. He came cheap."

"Somebody must say no," Deacon said.

### R.I.P. When All is Said and Done

"No isn't an answer the Clearing House accepts. They can make a death appear to be a suicide, or a drowning, a botched hold-up that ends in a slaying. Lots of options, and I have a list of names of those who tried to say no. That's part of the package I can bring.

"They don't take any chances. When that guy Bobby got killed they sent operatives to St. Louis to check on his background. They even searched his trailer."

The Professor stared at the flickering lantern. "You mentioned in the car this organization is headquartered in Singapore. Who runs it?"

"There's a group of six men with a woman at the top. She carries the title of Sovereign. I don't have names of the seven, and don't know how power transfers when someone gets old and dies."

Mike rose. At six and a half feet, and well over two hundred pounds, he towered over Joe. "So the world's got evil and is a corrupt fucking place—nothing new there. Let's keep this simple. I want to find out who killed Bobby, and do something about it."

The Professor slapped the end of his cane on the floor. "Dammit, Mike, there are so many moving parts we have to consider."

With hands folded, Joe bent over. "I shot Bobby with the gun I gave you guys. I told the Professor about it being an accident. The Clearing House wanted some information, and they gave me the job to get it. I never killed anyone in my life—till that day."

In his high-pitched voice, Joe said, "I regret it. It can't be undone."

Roof tiles rattled and moist air poured through breaks in the windows, as the wind picked up.

Mike said, "I need to roll up my truck windows—be back in a minute." He turned as he walked out the door. "Joe, feel free to grab that last hamburger."

Mike rolled up the driver side window, and then reached under the front seat and pulled out a .38 caliber revolver, and a 9mm semi-automatic handgun.

Mike reentered the room with a gun in each hand, and another shoved in his belt. Joe was still seated facing the Professor to his right, and Deacon to his left.

Mike handed the revolver to the Professor and the 9mm to Deacon, and then stepped toward Joe. "I'm sure it doesn't matter to you or anyone else in this damn town that Bobby was a right guy. He'd lend you money if he had it, and always covered your back in a fight. His name is never going to appear on the side of a building, show up on a plaque, a signpost, or be bragged about. Five fucking people showed up at his funeral."

Mike released the safety on his handgun. "You kidnap and drug a guy off the street, and then claim his death an accident. You must be kidding!"

With his hands gripping the seat of his chair, Joe stared at Mike. "I'm sorry."

"Save that regret for your Maker, maybe it will carry some weight."

Mike aimed his gun at Joe, while signaling the Professor and Deacon. "We fire at the same time, wipe our fingerprints off these metal chairs, grab the lanterns and bags of food, and take off. We'll dump all the guns in the Potomac, and head home. We'll leave his body here. The cops, if they bother to investigate, will conclude his gangster friends caught up with him. Later we'll get a bottle of something and celebrate."

Joe bent over and began to mumble.

The Professor shouted. "Before anyone fires, I have something to say."

Deacon agreed. "Go ahead, Professor. We're in this together."

The Professor set his revolver on the floor next to his chair, and then stood. "Sure, we want someone to pay for Bobby's murder. Blowing away Joe might make us feel better in the moment, but society has a way of dealing with this. Crime and criminals must be fought through laws and due process. That means police, courts, juries, judges, wrapped in written and case law. Otherwise a community descends into chaos where everyone grabs a knife or gun to settle a score. This requires much more from us. Joe admits he shot Bobby, gave us the gun he used, and wants to talk to the police. We can take this to Sergeant Craft. The criminal system will have more than enough to convict Joe of Bobby's murder. Plus,

Joe says he has mountains of hard evidence against that gang from Singapore. Put that on the plate, and we can help bring down corrupt politicians, judges, global fat cats, and who knows what else when we start to unravel that giant web. That's a huge contribution to society we lose if we shoot Joe and walk away."

Joe started to rise out of his chair, Mike waved his gun, and Joe slumped back down.

The Professor continued. "And let's not forget Rebecca. She knows I met with Joe tonight. Plus, she did have an indirect role in Bobby's death. Mike, are you up to killing a woman? Once we start shooting, when do we stop? You want street justice, and that's so damn limited."

"Sometimes street justice is all they leave you. I didn't go to college like you and Deacon. I was in the Army killing people in the second Gulf War, and getting wounded. I've been 'working class' my whole life. You remember, Deacon, the kind of folks that built and held our neighborhood together."

Mike glanced at the flickering lantern. "I'm the guy they make fun of in New York, out in Hollywood, or here in Washington. Fuck them. Now you want us to give this over to the corrupt sons-of-bitches running this place. Professor, you sampled them at Cassy's Café the other day. Did you spot any good guys there?"

The Professor leaned on his cane, and faced Mike. "You're right, this town, hell the country and beyond is full of arrogant, self-righteous people with way too much money and power. And yet someone must stand up and shout—STOP. We can do that with Joe's testimony and his evidence. Then you add Rebecca stepping forward, and we put an end to Senator Hodge's bid for the Presidency and maybe a lot more."

"This town has no interest in the kind of justice you're talking about. First, they don't give a shit about Bobby—a nobody from nowhere. A guy living in a trailer out there in fly over country that got dead in their town. Then this business about us helping tear down a corrupt system with Joe's information. Are you kidding? There's no appetite here, or any other big-shot city for tearing down a system that keeps them in their million-dollar mansions, yachts, and power. Who's going to help with all this? The FBI, Big Media, Big Shot Globalists? I read and keep up to date. Demons have taken root in all those places. Instead of exposing this shit, they'll bury it and us with it."

The Professor held up his hand. "Let's hear from Deacon, and let majority rule. If he agrees with you, then we blast Joe and head home. If he agrees with me, we take Joe to the cops and believe this country still capable of fighting corruption and producing justice for Bobby."

Mike nodded at Deacon. "It's up to you, brother. How should we respond to the murder of our old friend?"

Deacon rose with the gun in his right hand. "Joe, how are you holding up?"

"I'll let you know in a few minutes."

Deacon glanced around the room. "I'll bet Saint Catherine's was really something back in the day."

It began to rain. Deacon gazed out the window as the water splashed off the hoods of the cars and rolled down the cracked and broken concrete, pooling at the bottom of the driveway. "There's something calming about a soft rain. Don't you think?" He then pointed at the flickering lantern. "Before we head back to St. Louis, we'll get our money back."

Deacon paused a moment, and then said, "Now let's talk about justice—the biggest and slipperiest idea in any language or culture. Once you start packing that word like you own it you grant yourself license to do anything. That idea should come with a warning—'handle it with care."

Deacon faced Mike. "We both learned a long time ago that justice is in God's hands. Sure, we have an obligation to address wrong doing, and hold people accountable. That's why the three of us came to Washington. The question facing us is pursuing a path of greater good. I understand you wanting to kill Joe, and leave it there. The problem is that leaves too much of our obligation to justice incomplete."

"Then fuck justice, and wrap this in revenge. It's just a damn word."

"I'm sure if we get Sergeant Craft involved, Joe gets charged with killing Bobby and we also get to strike a blow at evil out there. And Joe will face God for Bobby's murder. I'll call Sergeant Craft and let him know what's going on. And we'll get Rebecca to meet us at the police station. I loved Bobby and believe he would prefer it that way."

Mike pointed at Joe. "Don't forget, if this bastard spills his guts and causes a lot of trouble for this Clearing House organization, they'll eventually find out the role we played in that. It sounds like they take things personal and don't mind killing people. Do we want that badass group pissed off at us? Maybe we spend the rest of our lives looking over our shoulders. Are you guys ready for something like that?"

Deacon signaled Joe he could stand up. "Of course, you're right. Turning Joe over has its risks. We could end up in somebody's crosshairs. Regardless of the danger, standing against corruption and evil is a fight I'm willing to make."

The Professor handed Mike his gun. "If our decision takes time off my life, it's time I'm willing to give. I can't think of a better cause. I agree with Deacon."

Mike locked the safety on his gun. "Go ahead—dream your dreams. You guys are counting on a Never Never Land producing real justice. Good luck with that shit. And Deacon, this Sergeant Craft character might be as corrupt as any of them. And don't count too much on that higher authority stepping in and making this all right. We haven't seen much evidence of that…*have we*? I hope Bobby understands this damn decision."

Mike collected his guns and headed toward the door. "The problem is you guys aren't mad enough."

Deacon reached Sergeant Craft around twelve-thirty Sunday morning, and told him he had the murder weapon and confessed killer of Bobby, along with a huge backstory. They agreed to meet at the police station in an hour.

Joe called Rebecca and she agreed to head over to the police station and share her part of the story.

The Professor drove Joe to the police station, while Mike and Deacon followed in the truck.

Mike swerved on to Indiana Avenue NW and glanced over at Deacon. "I'll bet Joe deals his way out of the murder charge. Or, he's found hanging in his cell. Or, maybe dies of some kind of food poisoning in jail. This town, these people, maybe the world doesn't weigh things the way we used to in the neighborhood. Standards were different, you were held accountable by your parents, neighbors, schools, and even the fucking media and government were basically honest. Let's face it, whatever we were—we ain't any more."

"Mike, I think Sergeant Craft will get after this. I've talked to him on the phone a bunch of times, and he's a serious man. He told me he grew up in a neighborhood like ours. He cares, and would love to round up those corrupt bastards in D.C. and elsewhere. This will lead somewhere good. We owe God our best effort to find and live with His justice."

"You got a lot of faith."

"Faith is the one thing I've never given up on. I thank Sister Annunciata for that strength."

Mike laughed, as he pulled into the police parking lot. "Who knew all those beatings from her served a purpose."

Joe and Rebecca were still meeting with Sergeant Craft and his people, when Mike, Deacon, and the Professor arrived back at their motel around three o'clock Sunday morning.

## The Way Home

Sunday at twelve-thirty, after dropping off the Professor's rental car, Mike, Deacon, and the Professor headed to the Basilica of the National Shrine of the Immaculate Conception, the largest Catholic Church in North America. It was founded in 1920, and designated by the Church as a sanctuary of prayer and pilgrimage.

Deacon stepped out of the truck, and glanced at the back seat. "With your game leg, why don't you wait here. We'll be back in an hour. I want to take a quick visit before heading home."

The Professor nodded. "I'll do the virtual tour."

Deacon headed to a huge gray and white stone tower. "The Knights' Tower, built with Knights of Columbus money from all over the country. It's the second highest structure in Washington behind the Washington Monument. There's nothing like it back home."

Mike shrugged. "I guess we got passed over again."

Twelve o'clock services were going on when Mike and Deacon entered the Basilica. Deacon dipped his fingers in the holy water and made the sign of the cross, and then gazed at the majesty of the Trinity Dome: its colorful mosaic depicting the Holy Trinity, the Virgin Mary, and a procession of saints. Mike wandered around, snapping a picture here and there while collection baskets passed from pew to pew. Deacon edged toward the pews and dropped twenty dollars in a basket. When the priest began to distribute communion, they left.

Once outside, Mike lit a cigarette, and said, "You could cram twenty Saint Pius X churches inside that building. Maybe we had the wrong saint pulling for us back then. I wonder if the folks running this place know or care what happened to our old parish, or the neighborhood. Never mind—I know the answer."

Deacon glanced back at the Basilica. "Let's head over to Rosary Walk."

A couple of minutes later, Mike and Deacon shared a bench facing a massive Carrara marble spiritual scene of the Fatima miracle. A short distance to their left was a full size marble crucifix of Christ on the Cross. Layers of lush green grass and colorful plants surrounded everything. Trees provided shade; a breeze spread the sweet smells of late spring, while noisy cardinals and blue jays flapped and skirmished in the treetops.

Mike pointed at a pair of white doves snuggled together on a bench across the way; he suggested they were taking in the sights like a couple of tourists.

Deacon watched three bright orange butterflies the size of silver dollars circle the Fatima statue and disappear into a thick row of dark-red roses, and then said, "I prayed for Pete and Mary. I asked God to help and keep them safe."

"I'll put an Amen to that."

Deacon then waved at a couple of elderly nuns, and said, "I'm glad Bonnie has my rosary. When she meets up with Bobby, he'll recognize it. That's the rosary they gave us at First Communion."

Mike put his arm around Deacon. "By now they've already gotten together. I'll bet Bobby is walking around up there with your rosary in his pocket."

Mike got up. "Let's head back, partner. I'll send Steve and Gary a text that we're finished."

While they were gassing up the truck, the Professor handed Deacon and Mike each a small gift-wrapped box. Inside was a gold pocket watch he purchased at Cato's jewelry store a few days earlier. Their three names were inscribed on the back; below the names in larger font was the Greek word Philia, for friendship.

They left Washington around two-thirty Sunday afternoon. Mike figured the drive would be about fourteen-hours, plus a couple stops for food and gas. Along the way, conversation covered baseball (they were all fans of the Cardinals) gardening, cars from the Sixties, and even ancient Greek and Roman history.

Eight-thirty, Monday morning, they were around seventy-five miles from St. Louis, on Old Hwy. 67. Deacon called his wife, and told her he would be home on Tuesday.

Mike honked at a speeding pickup, and then glanced back at the Professor. "So you wrote a book about Aristotle. Do you think he would have voted with me back there in Washington?"

"Wisdom never grows old, and Aristotle is one of the wisest men in history. He told us a successful political community's foundation is built on the exercise of virtuous reason so it can distinguish just from unjust—having a common sense of fairness and justice. From there we get laws, people who administer the laws, and the kind of political leadership that maintains good government. Virtuous reason anchors everything important."

Mike laughed, and said, "So virtuous reason is the tonic that will fix things. Where is it? It's not in Washington or these other big-shot cities. It's either hiding or isn't relevant anymore."

"I'll admit we're a long way from anything resembling good government. Aristotle has provided us with a roadmap, and I believe what we did back there will be a step in the right direction. I don't think Aristotle would have sided with you."

"Come on, Professor, wise men are always willing to learn. That's what makes and keeps them wise. Let Aristotle hang around Washington and a few other big cities and who knows what he would have done back there. I'm saying—you might be surprised. And Deacon, even God whacks folks now and then. Ask Sodom and Gomorrah."

"But we're not God."

Mike was pondering Deacon's comment when he spotted a small figure hobbling on the side of the road. He slowed the truck and saw it was a skinny tan Cairn terrier holding up its left front paw as it ran along the grassy roadside. He drove a couple hundred feet and parked, and then hurried toward the injured creature. Deacon and the Professor followed.

## STORY TWO

"Make your damn bet," Jerry said.

Kevin pushed his stack all in. "It will cost you another three dollars."

Jerry matched it. "Full house, kings over fives. Beat that, you son-of-a-bitch."

Kevin tossed his cards. "Take it."

Jerry raked in the pot as he glanced around the small wooden table in the corner of his parent's hot, humid basement. "Whose deal is it?"

Kevin took a last puff, and then stuffed out the butt. "You got all the money—game over."

It was August, 1950. Jerry Sizemore, Kevin Lancy, Brian Freymann, Jim Covington, and Luke Gherardi, were all fifteen years old and heading into their sophomore year at Riverview Gardens High School, located just outside, St. Louis, MO.

School started in two weeks, and the conversation shifted to which teachers they expected to get for math, science, gym class, etc.

Brian said, "Gym class is always a fucking waste of time, except for the jocks."

Luke mentioned his older brother Seth had been shipped overseas to fight in the Korean War. Musial was having another great year at the plate, but they agreed the Cardinals had no chance to win the pennant.

After a few minutes, Jerry leaned back in his chair. "Let's head over to Patty's Pizza. It's on me."

Brian shook his head. "Hell, that's a three-mile walk."

"It's a mile if we cut through the cemetery."

Jim got up and headed toward the basement door. "Fuck it, I'm going home."

Kevin followed Jim out the door.

Jerry laughed. "You guys aren't going to let the dead keep you from Patty's great pizza."

Brian rose from his chair. "I'll take my chances for a free pizza."

Luke picked up his lighter. "Sure, why not. What can the dead do to you?"

The temperature had hit ninety-six degrees, and was still simmering in the mid-eighties as they headed out the basement door a little past one-thirty, Friday morning.

Jerry signaled for quiet. "Don't get my dog excited. He'll bark and wake my parents, or my little brother Frank."

Fritz, the family's large German shepherd, ignored them as they climbed over the rattling chain-link fences separating the backyards. There were no street lights or sidewalks in this working-class neighborhood that sprung up with GI loan money after World War II. The small wooden-frame ranch homes measured about eight-hundred square feet, and cost ten-thousand dollars.

Dressed in white T-shirts, jeans, and tennis shoes, they clung to the curb as they headed down Cameron Blvd. Dogs barked here and there, and an occasional porch light had been left on. Entrance to the cemetery lay four blocks and a dash across busy Riverview Boulevard. At the corner of Cameron and Ross Circle, they ducked behind a row of thick overgrown hedges at the approach of a police car. They hugged the ground, sweat pouring and mosquitos biting, as the patrol car rolled by. After it swung down the next corner and disappeared, they sped up their pace.

Jerry pointed at a white-shingled house on Tay Avenue, as they hurried along. "Gary Fullmore lives there. I beat the son-of-a-bitch up last year. He hasn't bothered me since."

"He's an asshole," Brian said.

Luke slowed as they passed the house. "He does have a cute sister named Jaimie."

Jerry grinned. "I'd like to get to know her."

They crossed Dunkel Circle, and slowed down a little. The Bulger House had lights on, and they heard lots of screaming as they passed.

"I'd hate to live under that roof. I feel sorry for the twins Jennie and Sue," Brian said.

Riverview Boulevard was busy with speeding cars and long-haul trucks. The cemetery entrance stood right across the street. They waited till a break in the traffic, and then ran across.

Their T-shirts, soaked with sweat, clung to their skinny frames as they pushed at the locked metal gate of the cemetery entrance.

Brian swatted a mosquito as he glanced at Jerry. "Come on, you owe us a pizza."

Luke emerged from behind a pair of nearby snowball bushes. "We can squeeze through over here."

Eternal Rest Cemetery opened in 1848 with the burial of a twenty-eight-year-old poet and song writer named George Franklin who had died from Gout. The next day Mike McMillan arrived, a forty-year-old drunk who fell off a wagon and got his neck run over by one of the wheels. He left a wife and five small children to fend for themselves. And so it went sinners and saints alike for the past hundred years. Some burials got mentioned in the papers, drew large crowds, tears, and speeches, while others got dumped in silence at county expense.

The full moon cast welcome light as Jerry, Brian, and Luke studied the forest of weathered gravestones and markers.

Luke took a deep breath. "OK, Jerry, where do we go from here?"

"I ain't been here since we buried my Uncle Frank seven years ago. Let's follow the road that started at the entrance gates and see where it takes us."

"I wonder who came up with the idea these folks are resting. That's crazy," Brian said.

Jerry laughed. "It's one big family we all get to join sooner or later."

"I don't look forward to spending eternity with bums and trash."

"Depends on how you treat this life."

They marched side-by-side, following the blacktopped road as it wound its way through the graveyard.

Luke ran toward a toppled gravestone. "Hey, guys, take a look. It says his name is Jersey Smith, born 1760, and died 1850. He could have been in the Revolutionary War, and met General Washington."

Brian rubbed off some of the stone's dirt. "Damn, ninety-years old, a real old-timer for those days. He might have fought and killed Indians. Or maybe he got killed by an Indian."

Jerry shoved the stone upright. "Regardless, let's straighten his grave marker."

Brian and Luke held the headstone, while Jerry packed dirt and a few rocks to give it support from behind.

After they finished, Brian asked, "Should we say a few words over his crusty old bones?"

Jerry glanced back, as he headed toward the blacktopped road. "Help yourself." .

Jerry lit another cigarette as they walked along. Suddenly they heard an explosive pop-pop-pop, followed seconds later by—bang. The noise came from the direction of the neighborhood.

Luke grabbed Jerry by the arm. "That's no car backfire."

Jerry took a drag. "This place might soon be getting a new customer. I hope it isn't anybody we know."

Brian, a little shaken, suggested they head back.

Jerry grinned. "We ain't cops, we ain't witnesses, and we sure ain't got any medical training. Why the hell would we go back? Besides, we still got a pizza to get."

Even with a full moon parts of the cemetery stayed pitch-black. They heard sounds of squirrels jumping tree limbs, or rabbits dashing toward the safety of the nearest patch of bushes. Where the road made a sharp turn, Brian swore he spotted a shadow moving amongst nearby oak trees.

Luke chided Brian. "We got a full moon, maybe it's a damn werewolf."

Jerry tossed a rock in the direction of the trees. "Come on out, Mr. Werewolf." After fifteen or twenty seconds of silence, they continued on.

Later they came across a larger-than-life-size marble statue of a man smiling atop a stone mausoleum with arms stretched out as if he were embracing the world.

Jerry ran over and read the name, Stephen "Big Boy" Aldridge. "This guy used to be our U.S. Senator. He pulled strings in Washington for over thirty years."

Brian asked, "Was he a saint or sinner?"

"My dad hated him, definitely a sinner that never got caught."

Luke responded. "Lots of people still praise him. They named a school and library after him."

Jerry shook his head. "I trust my dad's instincts. The media covered up a lot of stuff this guy did because he championed causes they approved of. They say he died of a heart attack while messing with a prostitute. If you believed Sister Annunciata, the wise get their reward and the wicked their comeuppance. I'll bet he's catching hell somewhere."

Brian drew their attention to a black rosary strung on the handle of the mausoleum door. "Somebody thinks his soul still needs help."

Jerry ran his thin sweaty fingers over the rosary beads. "Who knows, it might do him some good."

Half-way through the cemetery, about thirty feet on the left, Brian noticed signs of a fresh grave. He ran over and saw a lawn-level stone atop the soft ground. It read: *Susie Weiss, 1895-1950.*

Brian called to his friends. "Ain't this the lady who worked at the school cafeteria last year?"

Luke read the name. "I remember her, plump, with short gray hair pulled back in a bun—always smiling. I wonder what happened. According to this she was fifty-five years old. I think she lived alone in those apartments over on Diamond Drive. I wonder if she left any brothers, sisters, or cousins around."

Jerry pointed to the statue of the senator off in the distance. "An arrogant bastard is noticed by everyone passing by, while this nice lady lays here in obscurity. It's not fair. I'll bet she led a better life than he did. Somewhere else, I'm sure that's being taken into account right now."

Jerry dropped to one knee and made the Sign of the Cross. "I heard she liked going to the zoo. Why don't we do a fundraiser and make a donation to the zoo in her name. Will you guys help me?"

Brian asked, "How would we pull this off?"

"The ladies in the cafeteria will know if she's got family. If she does, I'll tell them what we have in mind, and maybe get their help. If she doesn't have family, then we'll see it gets done ourselves."

Luke asked, "Who would contribute?"

"We'll set a dollar target, and then organize a fund raiser at school, around our neighborhood, and at her apartment complex. We could get it mentioned in the local papers. I don't know all the details. It's something I'm going to do for the nice lady. Maybe we get some kids from the school band to play something when the donation is made to the zoo. Come on guys, this could be fun."

Luke and Brian faced each other for a moment, and then agreed to help out. They shook on it, and then proceeded down the blacktopped road.

Brian tossed a pebble. "If we hadn't stopped along the way, we would be eating now."

Jerry glanced around the cemetery. "It's been worth it. Look at all the interesting people we've met. I've gained a new perspective on life by meeting the dead up close and personal. Someday we're going to have our own plots. I'm sure they could even clear out a patch of weeds around here for you two guys."

Brian slapped Luke's shoulder. "The man's trying to be funny."

"I'm kidding. Yet when you think about it you gain more respect for the time between now and then."

"You're getting too fucking deep for me. I just want a pizza," Brian said.

"All right, no more stops. It shouldn't be too much further."

The road twisted and turned, as they passed old and new dead. Brian spotted more shadows behind the trees. It began to wear on Luke's nerves.

Luke stopped. "Until I'm dead, this is the last fucking time I spend in a boneyard—day or night. Not for pizza, not for money, not for anything."

Jerry laughed, and then pointed at a small white-stone building about fifty yards ahead. The door stood open and a glimmering light spilled from a side window.

"Maybe someone's in there praying?" Jerry said.

Brian raised his voice. "At this time of night! The gates are locked, so whoever it is must have broken in like us."

Luke whispered to Jerry, "Let's get the hell out of here. At best it's a security guard, which means we have a lot of explaining to do. At worst—who knows."

Jerry headed toward the building. "I have to see who is in there, and why. You guys can wait here if you want."

They hesitated a few seconds, and then caught up with Jerry.

As they got closer, they noticed the building's white stones had no wear on them, as if the construction had been recent. The tan-tiled roof also looked new. The single-story structure had no more than a thousand square feet. Twenty feet in all directions from the building lay rows of thick green grass. Red roses bordered both sides of the cast-iron door, soaking the surrounding air with a sweet aroma.

Jerry pushed the door open a little wider and walked through, followed by Luke and then Brian. The solid oak floor was without a scuff mark. The ceiling looked about fifteen-feet high, and the walls paneled and stained a deep-red mahogany. At the front of the otherwise empty room sat a wooden bench. The metal door snapped shut behind them.

A dark-haired woman wearing a gray robe stood at the other end of the room with her back to them. The dim light seemed to be emanating from her, filling the small space with a soft glow. The woman pointed to the bench.

Led by Jerry, they marched nervously to the front of the room. Jerry sat in the middle, Brian a couple feet to his left, and Luke to his right near the edge of the bench. Although steamy outside, the room felt cool and comfortable.

Luke appeared ready to run for the door, when Jerry held up a cigarette. "Ma'am, do you mind if we smoke?"

The woman turned and gazed at Jerry. She was light-skinned, with dark-brown eyes. Her shoulder-length brunette hair shined in the dim light. She appeared to be in her early twenties. A bluish-green emerald ring sparkled on her right hand. She signaled it was OK to smoke.

After a couple of drags, and feeling more relaxed, Jerry asked, "Why are you here this late at night? Are you praying for someone?"

Jerry added, "Even in this neighborhood, it's unsafe for a woman to be out alone at night. Like it or not, the world is full of bad guys and real live boogeymen. You need to be careful."

"Yes, the world has not lived up to expectations," She said in a soft voice. "And, why am I here? I've come to share, console, and provide guidance."

A slight plea showed on her face. "Make the most of this special opportunity. The world you live in continues to have challenges."

She waved her arm, and the wall at the front of the room became a large window. She snapped her fingers and the movement of star clusters, constellations, clouds of stardust, and shooting comets could be seen through the window. Then galaxies, Jerry recognized Andromeda, and the Milky Way. On and on it went, supernovas, spectacular meteor showers, and then nothing but blinding light.

"There's no beginning or end. Yet, know you're an important part of all this," she said.

With Jerry in the middle, he and his friends clumped together on the bench. They were well into their second smoke when the wall returned to its original form.

Luke whispered. "How did she do that?"

Jerry shrugged, and then asked, "Why are we important? We're average high school kids. Hell, Luke's done the sixth grade twice, he's even below average."

Luke punched Jerry in the arm. "Don't tell her that."

"I'm willing to bet she already knows."

She leaned forward. "You're important because each of you has been given a very special gift called a soul—your link to eternity and its wonders. Everyone you passed in the cemetery is on their second journey."

"What's beyond the blinding light?" Jerry asked.

"There are multiple paths and places in the second journey, measured by how you spend your time here. Whether you experience what's beyond the light is up to you."

Jerry nodded. "Who are you? Where are you from?"

"I'm from here, and now everywhere. Think of me as a messenger and what you've seen is a small part of reality."

She waved her hand and snapped her fingers causing the wall to come alive again. This time it displayed masses of bodies moving, shoving, and pushing each other in a vast space of semi-darkness. Men and women, old and young pushed and shoved as they grunted, barked, cried, and screamed in pain. Faces bent and contorted; some prayed while others cursed. A rotten-egg odor filled the room.

Brian gripped the bench. "God damn that place!"

Jerry nodded. "I think you got the picture. That's the place none of us want to end up."

After watching for a few seconds, Luke closed his eyes.

The woman studied their reactions, and then snapped her fingers, causing the wall to reappear.

Hands shaking, Brian borrowed a cigarette from Jerry. "That's the scariest and smelliest horror picture show I've ever experienced. I wonder how it ends."

"I think you saw the ending," Jerry replied.

Luke started to rise. "Those moans and smell drove me crazy. Let's get the hell out of here."

Jerry prevented Luke from getting up. "Stay put—this is important. I got a feeling there's a whole lot more coming."

Jerry asked, "Ma'am, what additional things do you want to show or tell us?"

She snapped her fingers, and the wall came alive with a giggling, laughing family sleigh riding down a steep hill, then it switched to flocks of honking geese soaring over a sparkling-blue lake, then noisy crowds shuffling up and down Manhattan's famous Broadway Boulevard with bright multi-colored lights bursting off the sides of buildings, then a thin woman with two small children gathered around a simple table eating, followed by a half-starved dog chained to a post wailing in the freezing cold, then two men with guns chasing another man down an alley, then a bloody body lying in a stairwell, then a fat man standing on the street munching caviar while another man lay in front of him in the gutter, then an old man lying silent in a bed surrounded by nurses, then large crowds of men, women, and children kneeling and praying—and on it went.

When she felt they had seen enough, the wall reappeared and the room returned to its dim light and stillness. She waited for a response.

Jerry glanced at his friends, and then spoke up. "That's our world. The beautiful, the bad, the challenged, and the very, very, wicked. It's the way we make and live it."

Brian appeared confused. "Ma'am, how are you doing all this? Is this some kind of trick?"

Jerry elbowed Brian. "It's as real as we are."

Brian asked the lady, "Why are you showing all this?"

"The light is always on, and the door open. You walk through on your own. What you do with the information is up to you."

Jerry thought a moment. "Ma'am, what you've showed us is pretty heavy stuff. What advice do you have to help me and my friends better understand all of this? I want to avoid missteps."

"Pray for wisdom, and act on the insights it provides. Search your soul—assistance is available. It is there to help you earn eternal happiness with your Maker."

The woman held out a gold pocket watch hanging on the end of a long chain. "Listen to it tick away the seconds. One day you'll realize your life took five minutes. This cemetery is filled with people once young like you, and some treated their time on earth as if it would last forever. Many have squandered their opportunity. Value each day, and show something for it. Trust me; there is a reward for those who manage their time with wisdom."

She pointed toward the door as it swung open. "We may see each other again."

Brian and Luke scrambled toward the open door, while Jerry stayed a second to gaze at the Lady: her piercing brown eyes, rich-dark hair, flowing robe, and enchanting smile. That alluring picture would stay fixed with him forever. The door closed as soon as he joined his friends outside.

Jerry checked his watch, and it showed a little after five o'clock, it would be light soon.

Luke started walking. "Let's head on back, and forget the pizza. I want to get out of here before we run into any security guards."

Jerry lit another cigarette as they walked along. "A pizza and security guards are trivial in light of what we've experienced."

After a couple hundred feet, Brian said, "She had me scared for a while, but the more I think about it she must have had something rigged up we didn't see. I'll bet her and a camera crew are parked somewhere around here. That couldn't have been real."

Luke nodded agreement. "It's a hell of a story we can share. I'll get Kevin and his brother Bill over here—maybe charge them. They'll get a kick out of this."

"You guys are so damn ignorant," Jerry yelled.

Brian glanced back. "What the fuck!"

The building, the rose bushes, even the thick green grass, all had disappeared.

Jerry ran back. Brian and Luke followed.

Jerry searched the area where a building stood less than ten minutes before. He saw no signs of a foundation, pieces of broken glass, splinters of wood, or stones lying about—just a lone gravestone.

Luke pointed to a large oak tree nearby. "I remember that tree, so this must be the same place. I didn't hear a thing. Buildings can't disappear."

Brian kicked at the ground. "I told you guys this place is creepy. Someone or something is fucking with us. Let's get the hell out of here."

Luke agreed. "Come on, Jerry, let's go."

Jerry focused on the grave marker about fifty feet away. "You guys go ahead. Wait for me outside the gate. I want to check something out first."

Luke and Brian ran off, while Jerry walked toward the gravestone.

The carving on the gravestone read: *Evelyn Bertelsman 1890 to 1913*. At the base of the gravestone lay three bright-red roses. Jerry knelt, uttered a few prayers, and then walked away. He glanced back, half expecting to see the building.

Fifteen minutes later, Jerry arrived at the gate entrance with his friends waiting on the other side.

Brian waved. "Hurry up, man, the traffic is picking up. We're going to have to dodge for our lives crossing Riverview."

Jerry, the tallest at a little over six foot, squeezed his skinny frame under the fence and joined his friends. They bolted across Riverview, and then headed back to the neighborhood.

Jerry glanced at Luke. "What happened to your elbow? It's all scraped up."

"I fell. No pizza, and a banged up elbow. Fuck this place. We figured the whole thing back there was a hoax. Maybe part of a scene from a Hollywood fantasy or horror movie."

"What were you doing?" Brian asked.

"I don't know. I felt something—still do. You guys saw the same things I did."

They walked a while, and then Jerry said, "Her name was Evelyn Bertelsman."

"Who are you talking about?" Brian asked.

"That's the name on the grave back there."

Luke rubbed his sore elbow. "Shit, that had to be a Hollywood prop. I'll bet there's no such person."

When they got to Dunkel Circle, they noticed a bunch of police cars, lights flashing, along with a large crowd gathered in front of the Bulger home. A friend of Luke's told him there had been a shooting. While they stood there, a body covered in a white sheet got shoved into a waiting ambulance. Jerry overheard a cop suggest a murder-suicide.

Jerry grabbed his friends. "Let's go home."

Sunday, after morning mass, Jerry shared the cemetery story with his parish priest, Father Johnson. The priest was skeptical, but knew Jerry from his first communion days and figured something might have occurred. Father Johnson quizzed Brian and Luke over the phone, and then drove Jerry to the cemetery Sunday afternoon.

After an hour, and no signs, Father Johnson put his hand on Jerry's shoulder. "Pray for guidance. Remember, your Guardian Angel is always there to help you. The Lord wants all of us to join Him."

School started on September 2$^{nd}$. Following up on his commitment, Jerry checked around and found the deceased cafeteria worker Susie Weiss had no living relatives. Her body had been discovered by a maintenance man at her building, and her death ruled accidental. The coroner concluded she died from a fall. Jerry shared his zoo fund-raising plans in Miss Weiss' name with Mr. Speed, the high-school principal. He agreed to help and they set a goal of one-thousand dollars. Jerry's dad donated ten dollars to the campaign.

Luke and Brian told the cemetery story to anyone who would listen. Brian added being chased by a gang of werewolves running amuck in the graveyard, while Luke insisted Hollywood had to be involved and the film would be out soon. When asked, Jerry acknowledged going to the cemetery and coming across Miss Weiss' grave. He wouldn't confirm anything else. Brian and Luke had reputations as big-time bull-shitters and their story fell by the wayside, replaced by more pressing news and stories concerning the growing Korean Conflict. A lot of recent graduates, including older brothers of many, had been shipped to that war against communist expansion. Jerry didn't share the cemetery story with his family.

Jerry reached his thousand dollar goal in thirty days, with contributions from the cafeteria staff, teachers, the student body, and a five-hundred dollar matching contribution from Whitney's Furniture, where Miss Weiss had bought a bedroom set a couple of years before. Jerry handed the thousand dollar check to zoo representatives at a special school assembly held in the gymnasium. An article mentioning Jerry's leadership in the fund-raiser appeared in the local newspaper. His fundraiser, along with other things, helped him get elected president of the sophomore class.

Jerry spent all his Saturdays in October and November at the Thomas Jefferson Library, repository of the archives of the two major newspapers St. Louis had in 1913. He researched death notices, and any articles that might supply additional information on Evelyn Bertelsman, the young woman mentioned on the gravestone. He hoped to find a photograph of her.

The Saturday before Thanksgiving, Jerry found what he wanted in the now defunct *St. Louis Sun*. Evelyn Bertelsman appeared in the death notices for Monday, March 17$^{th}$ 1913. Place of death listed as Mt. Saint Rose Sanatorium. Cause of death shown as chronic tuberculosis. Born October 12$^{th}$, 1890, and the only child of local industrialist Alois and wife Cecelia Bertelsman. The death notice didn't include a picture, so Jerry checked the society column for that day—and there she was. The column summarized her brief, active life, which included several black-and-white full-length photos. The smile, that hair, the tall slim-figure; no doubt the woman he and his friends had met in the cemetery. The article stated she graduated high-school in 1908, and had started college. She left in her freshman year after diagnosed with tuberculosis.

After reading the article, Jerry reached two conclusions: life's not fair and he would take her miraculous message seriously. He later shared the article about Evelyn with Brian and Luke. They weren't interested.

In December every house in Jerry's neighborhood had a Christmas tree shining through the small front window along with a string of outdoor lights wrapped around the house. Most front lawns included plastic reindeer, elves, Santa Claus, and snowmen helping celebrate the season. An older couple at the corner of Perthshire Avenue always erected a manger scene with a crib and baby Jesus. As soon as it got dark, the neighborhood lit up with bright blues, dazzling reds, and colorful shades of green, orange, yellow, and sparkling purples.

At Jerry's house, putting up the Christmas tree and outdoor lights took place on the first Sunday in December. The Scotch pine tree, strapped to the hood of their old Ford, always came from a Boy Scout lot a couple blocks away. Jerry and his dad put up the tree and strung the lights. His mom Dorothy and little brother Frank applied the ornaments and loads of silver tinsel. Mom did the decorations under the tree, including the nativity scene, while Jerry and his dad completed the outdoor work—a plastic Santa surrounded by a couple of reindeer. When finished, the family sat down to a snack of warm chocolate chip cookies and hot tea. The decorations kept up appearances expected in the neighborhood for this time of year.

As president of the sophomore class, Jerry helped erect and decorate the school's thirty-foot Christmas tree with the traditional nativity scene tucked under it. The weekend before Christmas, the high-school band toured the surrounding neighborhoods, playing and singing Christmas carols.

Christmas Eve at Jerry's house always included his Aunt Joan and Uncle Joe. They were childless, and enjoyed spending the time with Jerry and his younger brother Frank. They arrived around six-thirty, presents got opened around eight, and they left between ten-thirty and eleven. This year, along with other gifts, Jerry's dad gave his mom a dozen long-stemmed red roses. Christmas day started with a short drive to Saint Catherine's for services, followed by breakfast at a nearby donut shop. The rest of the day would be spent checking out his gifts, and finding out what his friends had gotten.

Jerry awoke around two o'clock Christmas morning and laid in bed thinking about Evelyn over there alone at the cemetery. The temperature had dipped into the mid-twenties; on those cold nights Fritz stayed in the basement. Jerry jumped out of bed at two-thirty, put on his jeans, shirt, and heavy cloth coat. He peered out his bedroom window and noticed it had begun to snow. He shoved on his stocking cap, grabbed one of the roses, and slipped out the front door. He planned to hike over to the cemetery, leave the rose at Evelyn's grave, sort of a Christmas present, and be back by five o'clock.

   A few Christmas lights were left on as Jerry tracked through the quiet neighborhood. He secured the rose on the inside pocket of his coat. He snuck into the closed cemetery at the same place he and his friends used back in August. As he ran along, he noticed Jersey Smith's gravestone had fallen over again. A few minutes later he stood next to a single grave in a snow-covered field. The cold frosty air brushed against his face as he laid the bright-red rose on the top of the gravestone. He bowed his head, recited several prayers, and then headed home. After fifty feet, he glanced back and saw his tracks in the snow leading up to and coming from the gravestone. However, the rose had disappeared. He clapped his cold hands and smiled.

   A little after five-thirty, Jerry climbed into bed pulling the thick warm blanket over him. He felt better about himself and life.

January 1951 arrived along with the previous semester grades. Once again, Jerry made the honor roll while his friends Luke and Brian stacked up their usual Cs, Ds, and occasional F. As president of the sophomore class, Jerry had a lot of administrative duties connected to the school including helping organize a memorial service for the first death in the Korean War of a recent graduate. A fellow named Lou Bravich, who had been on the school's wrestling team. He had been shot through the head by a sniper.

In February, Brian got suspended for a week for smoking at school. Jerry's brother Frank, now in the eighth grade, cracked his collar bone in a sledding accident. And Jerry broke up with his girlfriend Liz. In April President Truman replaced General MacArthur as commander of the troops in Korea, a move that pissed off Jerry's dad, and a lot of other folks. By then four graduates of Riverview Gardens had been killed in the war.

Jerry wanted more than a few pictures of Evelyn and a brief summary of her life from a newspaper column. Her spirit had reached out—he had to know more about her. She had been dead for almost forty years, so people she went to high school with would be in their late fifties. The newspaper article mentioned an aunt named Ruth Callahan. He hadn't decided whether he should share the cemetery story if he did meet up with anyone who knew her.

When summer arrived Jerry got a job as an usher at a local movie theater. He turned sixteen, and started to drive. For $75 dollars he bought a 1938 black Plymouth sedan with lots of rust and miles on it. Because it leaked so much oil, his dad made him park it in the street.

In between watching movies and hanging out with friends, Jerry learned Evelyn graduated from Incarnate Word Academy, an all-girls Catholic high school. Unfortunately, the school had closed in 1928. The local Diocese provided no help. Her family's address on Laclede Place had been torn down and replaced by an apartment complex during the 1940s. He then began searching for Ruth Callahan, the aunt. She would know things about Evelyn that no one else would. If alive she would be somewhere in her eighties.

He checked recent city phone directories, senior centers, and city death certificates with no luck.

On a Saturday in early August, Jerry decided to drive to Ironton and Fredericktown, a couple of small nearby towns to check their phone directories, and ask around for a Ruth Callahan. It was a long shot, but he had the day—work didn't start till six o'clock. Ironton turned out to be a bust. He then drove the fifteen miles to Fredericktown, arriving around twelve-thirty. City Hall had closed, so he decided to grab a quick lunch.

Jerry stopped at a soup-and-sandwich shop in a small brick building on Main Street. Above the entrance a neon sign flashed Green Frog Diner. The letter "g" in frog was burnt out. A note posted on the door indicated it was now under fifth generation management. Jerry slid into a booth by the window, and glanced around. There were about twenty dark-blue booths, and a soda counter with ten red stools. The brown-tiled floor was worn and cracked. As he peered out the window, he noticed dust buildup on the blinds. It looked like the place hadn't been remodeled in fifty years.

Jerry asked the young gal who took his order. "Is there a Ruth Callahan living around here? She would be an older lady."

She shrugged. "Don't know her. I'll ask the folks in the kitchen."

Five minutes later the server arrived with Jerry's ham sandwich, blueberry muffin, and root beer. "No one ever heard of her."

Frustrated, Jerry finished his lunch, and planned to head home.

As Jerry opened his car door, a woman shouted, "Young man." He turned and faced a short, middle-aged woman.

"I overheard you asking about a Ruth Callahan," she said.

Jerry nodded. "You know her?"

"Are you a relative, or something?"

"I'm not a relative. I'm researching the life of a young woman named Evelyn Bertelsman, who died about forty-years ago. Evelyn had an aunt named Ruth Callahan. I thought talking to her about her niece might provide insights into the kind of person this young gal was."

"So you're not a relative. Is this some kind of high-school project?"

Jerry thought a moment, and then took a deep breath. "It's not a school project. It would be hard to explain. You might not believe me if I told you how this all got started. Do you know a Ruth Callahan?"

The woman fished around in her purse, and pulled out a pencil and piece of paper. "Give me your name and telephone number. I'll check this out with the lady I think you're asking about. It's up to her if she wants to talk to you."

"I'd love to hear from her. Make sure she knows it's about her niece Evelyn."

On Thursday, in the last week in September, Jerry got a call around six-thirty in the evening from a Ruth Callahan who indicated Evelyn Bertelsman was her niece. She provided directions to an address outside Fredericktown, and agreed to meet Saturday morning at ten-thirty.

Jerry hung up and slapped his hands together. He had planned on shooting baskets Saturday morning at the school gym with Brian, Luke, and a few others. But talking to Evelyn's aunt would help him learn things he couldn't otherwise know. Jerry ran to his room and worked on a list of questions to make sure he asked. This might be the only chance he would have to talk to this lady.

Jerry's mom poked her head in his bedroom door. "What's got you so excited?"

"Mom, it's hard to put into words. I'm going to meet someone Saturday who might have very important information for me."

"Don't get mysterious. Who are you meeting, and what is it about?"

"It's just an old lady. And I'm not sure what it's all about. Don't worry, I'll be safe."

Arms folded, his mom replied, "Make sure you stay out of trouble."

Jerry gazed up at the ceiling. "I will."

Jerry rose at seven-thirty Saturday morning, had a quick breakfast of cold cereal, and then grabbed a white shirt, shined his shoes, and put on his black dress pants. He shoved a blue tie in his pants pocket as he walked out the door a little before nine o'clock. This gave him a little extra time in case he had any trouble finding the rural address.

A little after ten o'clock, a few miles outside of Fredericktown, Jerry found Old Jackson Road, and swung onto its narrow blacktopped lanes. After double checking his make-shift map, he figured the address should be about a mile away on his right.

The surrounding dense woods included elms, oaks, and walnut trees starting to display their fall burst of orange, red, and yellow colors. Tall grass and weeds bulged out from both sides of the road. Jerry dodged a large pothole, and then a box turtle. He jammed on his brakes and skidded twenty feet to avoid hitting a deer. A minute later he stopped in front of a rural mailbox with the number 224 posted on its side. He backed up and pulled onto a driveway made of broken white rocks leading to a small one-story wood-framed house. Jerry cut the motor, and gazed at the building. The gray-shingled roof looked beat up, its gutters packed with leaves. He figured it leaked. One side of the house showed a musty green buildup of mildew and mold.

Jerry's watch showed a quarter after ten. He put on his tie, and wondered whether he should sit and wait for fifteen minutes, or go up and knock. He noticed a couple of gray squirrels scramble across the roof. A few seconds later the front door swung open, and a skinny, gray-haired woman, with the aid of a cane, stepped onto the front porch wearing white sneakers and wrapped in a green terry-cloth bathrobe. She signaled for him to come in.

Jerry combed his short-cropped blond hair, grabbed his clipboard with several pieces of paper, and then headed toward the old lady. They introduced themselves, and then she led him inside and seated him at a worn gray couch. Jerry noticed to his left a broom leaning against the wall and a couple of dead roaches lying inside a dustpan. The room smelled like it had received a heavy dose of insect repellant.

Within arm's length sat a large plate of chocolate donuts, two cups, and a pot of steamy hot coffee atop a small wooden table.

Ruth pointed to the plate of donuts. "Grab one."

After pouring each a cup of coffee, she said, "How old are you?"

"I'm sixteen."

She clasped her small frail hands together. "Ah, to be sixteen again!"

She laid her cup on the table. "I hear you asked about my blessed niece Evelyn Bertelsman. No one has mentioned her name in over thirty years. I agreed to meet with you because I need to know why you asked, and what you want to know. Do you have an older relative, perhaps a classmate of hers?"

"You're going to have a tough time believing this."

"Try me."

"I met her…spirit."

She studied his face, and then refilled her cup of coffee. "Give me the details."

Over the next thirty minutes, Jerry shared what happened at the cemetery. Ruth's face perked up when Jerry mentioned the emerald ring, and the spirit's piercing brown eyes.

Ruth leaned toward Jerry. "I slipped that ring on Evelyn's finger right before they closed the coffin. I didn't even tell her parents. And yes, she had enchanting eyes. One color photograph of her exists, and I've got it. I don't know how you know those things, unless what you've told me is true."

Ruth grabbed her cane. The crusty wooden floorboards creaked as her pale, skinny frame moved around the room. Jerry noticed her cheeks showed a touch of rouge. She opened a desk drawer and pulled out a metal box, and then sat back down on the couch.

She held the box close to her chest. "We buried Evelyn in her own half-acre lot. Her parents are nearby. They couldn't cope with her death. Her dad's business fell apart, and my sister, her mom, took to the bottle. Evelyn was all they had or wanted, and both died within ten years of Evelyn. The only things left of the estate were old memories and a few pictures and documents."

She placed the metal box on the table, and poured herself another cup of coffee. "You've told me Evelyn has reached out to you in a profound way, and I believe you. Have you told your parents about her?"

"No. I haven't shared details with anyone except my parish priest."

"What about those two fellas with you at the cemetery? What stories have they told?"

"They ran around school telling everyone, adding werewolves, boogeymen, and Hollywood elements to the story. No one believed them, and I no longer discuss it with them. We weren't affected the same way. She shared a deep message, and I need to find out more about the messenger."

"Has she ever appeared again?"

"I haven't seen her, but have felt her presence another time."

"Tell me about it."

"I slipped into the cemetery last Christmas hours before it opened, and laid a red rose atop her gravestone. I hadn't gotten fifty feet when I noticed the rose had disappeared. A feeling came over me she had accepted the rose. I can't explain it any other way."

Ruth opened the metal box. "Red was Evelyn's favorite color, and red roses her favorite flowers. When she was eight, her and her mother planted a dozen red-rose bushes that bloomed from late spring to late September. They reached out with a sweet smell as you approached the house. It used to be such a great neighborhood. When I walked up those steps, a lot of the times Evelyn burst out the front door smiling and gave me a big hug. God I miss her."

Ruth wiped away a tear. "One day you'll wonder where all the years went. Time gets away from all of us."

Ruth handed Jerry a picture. "Here's Evelyn in her white dress and veil when she graduated eighth grade at Incarnate Word Academy. She got great grades, and was the most popular girl in her class."

Ruth handed him another picture. "Evelyn loved animals. That's her with her old dog Pepper. She was about sixteen then, and had that little terrier from the time he was a puppy. They used to run around the backyard chasing a ball or each other, laughing and barking as they went. You never forget those things. It broke her heart when Pepper passed away—she cried for days. I helped Evelyn bury him in a wooden box in their backyard. We recited a few prayers and laid roses on his grave. I'm sure his bones are still there."

Ruth commented as she handed Jerry other pictures, and then she held up a sheet of paper with writing on it. She scanned the document, and then began to cry. She laid the pictures back in the metal box, leaving the sheet of paper, yellowed with age, on top.

After closing the box, Ruth grabbed Jerry by the hand. "No one has asked about my niece in all these years. Young man, I believe my sweet Evelyn has reached out to you. What do you plan on doing about it?"

"I don't know. Her birthday is in a few weeks. I'll get a red rose and visit her gravesite."

"My caregiver drives me over to the cemetery on Evelyn's birthday. I'll have her push it back this year so the two of you can have your privacy."

Ruth handed Jerry the metal box. "I want you to have this. I'll be gone one of these days, and I don't want those contents ending up in a trash can, or for sale in some flea market. There's nothing else in this junk pile worth a lot. I believe you'll take good care of what's in there.

"On top you'll find a poem written by Evelyn while at the Infirmary run by the Sisters of Saint Mary. A nun found it the day she died and gave it to her mother. Don't read it till you get home."

Ruth reached for a donut. "I don't know where this goes. Maybe God has appointed her to work with your Guardian Angel? Something must have driven you here."

Ruth asked Jerry about his high school, his friends, teachers, and sports they played. She also learned a little about his family. She mentioned after the business failed, and the deaths of her sister and brother-in- law, she drifted around in low paying jobs until she ended up here around ten years ago. An old friend had left this place to her in her will. She told Jerry her state-sponsored caregiver named Linda dropped by three times a week to check on her and drive her to town for groceries and other items. On the other days the caregiver checked in on her by phone.

Ruth waved her hand in the air. "I used to live so grand. All I got is enough for burying money not far from Evelyn. Yesterdays pile up so fast, after a while all you're doing is looking back. It ain't much of a life."

Jerry took Ruth's number, and promised to take her for a drive up to the Green Frog Diner for lunch sometime during the coming Christmas holidays.

Ruth grew a smile. "I still put up a live Christmas tree every year, with the help of my caregiver. The manger scene and a couple of gold ornaments are from when I was a little girl. It takes me back, and makes me feel young again. The tree will be up the next time you're here."

Ten minutes later Jerry stood on the gray-wooden porch with the metal box under his arm. Ruth gave him a hug, and watched as he backed out of the driveway and disappeared up the road.

On the drive home, Jerry did a lot of thinking. He felt sorry for Ruth. She didn't seem happy or sad, just a person left with memories waiting to die. He wondered if he would end up alone and old at a farmhouse, apartment, or stacked up at a nursing home. Yet some died young like his Uncle Frank and Evelyn. His thoughts wandered back to Ruth's comment about Evelyn working with his Guardian Angel. Jerry repeated a few prayers, hoping guidance lay ahead.

When Jerry got home he shoved the metal box under his bed.

Jerry's brother walked in. "What are you hiding there?"

Jerry grabbed Frank by the shirt collar. "Don't touch it. And swear you won't tell Mom and Dad either. It's kind of strange, and they might not understand if I told them the whole story right now."

"OK, I swear."

It was Friday, October 12<sup>th</sup>, Evelyn's birthday. Jerry left school early and bought a dozen long-stem red roses at The Flower Shop. He wanted to get to the cemetery with three or four hours of light left in the day. He also brought her poem.

Jerry pulled through the front gate in his old Plymouth, and followed the blacktop road till he spotted Evelyn's grave marker in the distance. The temperature was mid-sixties with a slight breeze. Fall colors painted the surrounding trees and bushes in lively reds, yellows, and oranges, with a few lingering greens.

Jerry shoved the poem in his shirt pocket, clutched the roses, and tried to think of what he should say or ask as he approached the grave. He passed markers starting with names Jeramiah, Siegfried, Katherine, Laverne, and others. Some were young and others old when they arrived. It reminded him how thin the line between them and him.

Jerry arrived at Evelyn's grave as a large white dove circled overhead and then flew toward a band of tall oak trees. Other than the sound of birds from the tree tops and occasional rustle of leaves, it was silent. After laying the roses at the foot of her grave, Jerry sat, cleared his voice, and recited the fourteen-line poem about the gifts of life and soul, and obligations that come with those gifts. The white dove returned and perched atop Evelyn's gravestone. After he finished, Jerry folded the paper and put it back in his pocket.

Jerry glanced around the cemetery, and then addressed the dove. "That poem, those thoughts, they're something we should appreciate and live by. What we do with God's gifts? Have they been wasted, abused, or used to provide a return? And what should a return look like?"

He leaned closer to the dove. "Those aren't easy questions. Have I been called to do something special? Brian and Luke were there."

Jerry thought a moment. "Yeah, they kind of dismissed the whole thing. They're not bad guys, but they do waste a lot of time. I've never forgotten you waving the pocket watch and telling us we're all living on short-time.

"By the way, I met your Aunt Ruth the other day—a very sweet lady. We're going to get together again during the Christmas holidays. I wish I could do more for her."

At the mention of Ruth's name the dove lifted its head and flapped its wings.

When it started getting dark, Jerry excused himself and headed to his car. He glanced back and noticed the roses and dove had disappeared.

When he got home Jerry went to his room and reread the poem's magic several more times, and then put it back in the metal box. He laid on the bed thinking until his mom called him for supper.

The first week of December Jerry's family spent a warm Sunday outside putting up the Christmas decorations. Jerry waved at neighbors engaged in similar activities.

Jerry tapped his dad on the shoulder, and pointed at the end of the street where the Mastersons had mounted a sleigh and reindeer on their roof.

Jerry's dad glanced down the street. "They're trying to show off."

While he lined up the decorations, including a couple of new elves, Jerry thought about Ruth and his commitment. He planned to use a payphone to make the long-distance call to let her know when he would stop by and drive her to the diner for lunch. He'd get her a small gift, and share his recent experience with the white dove.

The following Tuesday Jerry phoned Ruth and got no answer. He phoned twice on Wednesday, and four times on Thursday with the same results. He remembered Linda, the caregiver's name. She would know if anything happened. He didn't have her last name, but knew she spent some of her free time at the diner.

After school on Friday, Jerry called the Green Frog Diner and asked for Linda.

The woman answering the phone, said, "I'll get her."

A moment later a woman's voice responded. "This is Linda. Who is calling?"

"My name is Jerry. We met a few months ago. I'm the young fella who asked about Ruth Callahan. We talked in the diner parking lot and you took my number."

"I remember."

"I've been trying to get hold of Ruth to take her to lunch sometime during this Christmas season. No one answers her phone."

Linda hesitated. "She died a couple of weeks before Thanksgiving. I stopped by to check on her and found her sitting on the couch in her green bathrobe—dead. The coroner listed it as a stroke. She'd been suffering from lung cancer, and a number of other old-age things. She's buried not far from her niece Evelyn. I don't think she had any living relatives. Her things and property go up for auction in January. She had a will and left everything to a nonprofit charity for cats and dogs."

"I'm so sorry she passed."

"I spent five years looking after that nice lady, and you were the first person to visit. She perked up after that, and talked about seeing you again."

Jerry thanked her for the information, and indicated he might come down for the auction.

Later in the day, Greg and Bill, a couple of Jerry's buddies, stopped by his house. The temperature was in the mid-forties, so they decided to walk the neighborhood and check out its holiday decorations. Most of the small houses blazed strings of bright reds, yellows, greens, and other colored lights. Many had decorative pieces to the front yard. They talked about school, sports, girls, and a recent fight Greg had with a guy they all disliked. They ran into a few friends along the way.

Jerry faced his friends as he lit a cigarette. "A lady named Ruth Callahan died a few weeks ago. She's buried over at the cemetery."

"Was she a relative, or friend of the family?" Greg asked.

"Nope, I met her once. She lived alone in an old beat-up shack outside Fredericktown."

"So what's the deal, did she get murdered or something?"

"She just got old and died. They found her sitting on her couch. I didn't hear about it till earlier today. She was a nice lady in her eighties that no one is going to remember. It makes you think."

"Makes you think about dying, or dying alone?" Bill asked.

"Both, I guess. I drank coffee and ate chocolate donuts with her a few weeks ago. She promised to show me her Christmas tree, and then we planned to do lunch sometime this month."

"How did you run into her?"

"It's a long story, but I'm glad we met. It's made me a better person to know her even a little. And that's worth a lot."

A rusty-red Chevy belching smoke from its noisy tailpipes pulled up, and Brian stuck his head out the driver's side window. "Let's crash a party over at Wendy's. I heard they got beer."

Greg jumped into the front seat. "It sounds like a plan." Jerry and Bill piled into the back and they took off.

Weighed down with glowing red, yellow, and deep-blue lights, shiny ornaments, and silvery tinsel, the Christmas tree sat as usual next to the front window—the shades pulled back. Mixed with the room's piney smell was the warm aroma of his mom's fresh-baked chocolate-chip cookies. It was Christmas Eve, Jerry's Aunt Joan and Uncle Joe had arrived with their packages a few hours before, and his brother Frank was eager to get at the presents. About twenty carolers from a local church had stopped out front around eight o'clock. After they sang *Silent Night,* and a few other standards, Jerry's dad ran out and gave them five dollars.

    They were too big for toys, so this year Jerry received a winter jacket from Mom and Dad, and a radio from his aunt. Frank got a leather wallet along with clothes, including several Cardinal sports items. Jerry and Frank bought their parents a camera. Jerry also gave his mom the gift he had bought for Ruth.

    Around eleven o'clock Aunt Joan and Uncle Joe headed home, while Jerry's mom cleaned up some of the discarded gift wrappings. At eleven-thirty, Jerry's dad turned out the lights, and reminded everyone they would be heading to church services the next morning.

    Jerry put on his new jacket and headed to the back porch for a quick smoke before bed. He leaned against the wooden railing and surveyed the quiet neighborhood. He took a drag as snow began to fall, the flakes illuminated by the back porch light. His first thoughts were another year and another Christmas come and gone. Ruth had been through a lot of these, yet was eager to experience another one. He added her name to his prayer list. He thought of Evelyn.

    After a few minutes, Jerry tossed his cigarette butt into the snow and lit another as he descended the steps into the backyard. He and his friends played kickball, tag, and catch here, sometimes after riding their bikes all day. It seemed like forever ago. Partially covered by snow, he noticed his old rusty bike on its side. He remembered what Ruth said about yesterdays piling up.

    Even at sixteen, Jerry began to feel he had accumulated quite a few of them—days gone and taken for granted.

Snowflakes pelted Jerry's face as he studied the night sky. He spotted a shooting star, and then another. He called Fritz and brushed the snow off his back as he led him into the basement. Before closing the door, Jerry took a last look around the backyard and skyward. From now on each day would count for something. He vowed not to flow nameless into eternity like so many others.

"As soon as it would start to snow, me, my brother Frank, and a couple of buddies would slap on our boots and gloves and drag our sleds to a big hill behind the church. Along the way, we'd fling a snowball at anyone passing by," Jerry said.

"It sounds like you had a great time," Kathy replied.

Jerry glanced up at Kathy. "Did you ever throw a snowball at anyone?"

"I tossed one or two, but just at people who deserved it. What I liked to do was build a snowman. Me and my sisters would dress him up and always name him Charlie. I used to watch from my bedroom window to make sure nobody pushed him over. Then it would get warm and Charlie would melt away. It felt like I lost a real friend. I learned early on nothing ever lasts."

"Everybody should love snow . . . and cats, dogs, and warm chocolate-chip cookies."

Jerry stared out the window as the big puffy flakes continued to fall. "I remember kicking a ball, playing tag, doing hide and seek. Kid fun has too short a life. You know what I mean?"

"They call it growing up, and taking on more responsibility."

"You're right."

Kathy laid her hand on Jerry's shoulder. "With all your awards, everyone has heard of and admires you. Many kids are healthier today because of you."

"I didn't do it alone. I have the greatest consultants anyone could ask for."

"Do you use some famous consulting group out of New York?"

"My Guardian Angel and spiritual friend Evelyn are there whenever I call on them. And I call on them a lot. It's much better than anything New York has available."

"Things have turned out pretty well."

Jerry gazed at the mounting snow. "We'll see. We're all waiting to see—aren't we?"

Kathy glanced at the clock. "It is nine o'clock, and lights have to be out in fifteen minutes." She pushed Jerry Sizemore in his wheelchair down the darkened hallway to his room.

Thirty-year-old registered nurse Kathy Novotny worked a twelve-hour shift, starting at ten o'clock in the morning, four days a week, at the hospice wing of Happy Gardens Hospital and Retirement Center, located outside Des Moines, Iowa.

The next morning, Kathy checked in at the front desk and passed through several sets of secured doors. At present, the hospice wing had thirty residents with an average age of eighty-seven. The typical length of stay was about sixty-eight days.

Kathy glanced at Mary, the nurse signing off her shift. "Did we lose anyone last night?"

"Grandma Kelly passed around two o'clock, and the mortuary people picked her up about an hour ago."

"Grandma served in the Women's Army Corp in World War II. By the way, how did our friend Jerry do last night?"

"We increased his morphine to deal with the pain from his stomach cancer. He's down to eighty-five pounds. He drank some orange juice. I stayed for a while, and he spent most of the time talking about old friends and his growing-up neighborhood. He also talked about some woman named Evelyn. He never married. Maybe she's an old lost love. It's kind of sad."

Kathy beamed. "I think she's more than an old girlfriend."

Mary grabbed her coat and headed toward the door. "Jerry got agitated last night with all the New Year's Eve fireworks going off. It's hard to believe its 2020 already. Time just gets away from us. Ten years ago I was a junior in high school—damn."

The staff was taking down the Christmas decorations as Kathy headed down the hall to check in on the residents. Betsy Hambrict, a new arrival, had become a screamer, so they had doubled her medications.

At eleven o'clock, the aides wheeled everyone down to the dining hall for lunch. Kathy had gotten into the habit of taking Jerry down there. Jerry had been moved to hospice from another wing about seven weeks prior. Since then he had lost twenty pounds. Bald, frail, he was just skin attached to bones. She knew it couldn't be long as she gathered him up and placed him in the wheelchair. On the way to the dining room, for the third time he told her his younger brother Frank had died in a car accident back in the Eighties. A day's activities for Jerry and everyone else included bingo at two o'clock in the big hall, and then color book drawing at four o'clock, dinner at five-thirty, and lights out by nine-fifteen. And more or less repeat the process the next day.

Around six o'clock Kathy stopped by Jerry's room to take his vitals. After she finished, he asked her to stay a moment. He wanted to share something important. She raised the front of his bed, and grabbed a chair and scooted up close.

In a soft voice, Jerry said, "There is another side after our time here. I've been given a glimpse of the good, the bad, and the ugly of it. I know it's there."

A smile grew on Jerry's face. "Where we land is always up to us. I told you last night I've had assistance along the way—we all have help available. We have to reach out and ask."

Kathy leaned forward. "You have a helper named Evelyn? You've mentioned her name before."

"Yes, yes, yes—she's real. Her full name is Evelyn Bertelsman, and she's helped guide me through a lot of rough patches over the years. I hope I've made enough right decisions to enter the next stage in good standing."

Kathy picked up a plastic container. "I'm sure you have. Would you like a drink of orange juice?"

Jerry shook his head, and then pointed to the desk. "No, thank you. I'd like you to get something out of the top drawer. Grab that sheet of paper."

She unfolded the paper. "This is a poem."

"Could you read it to me?"

"I'd love to."

After she finished, she folded it. "It's so lovely and inspiring. Did you write it?"

"Evelyn wrote it. I got it as a gift seventy years ago, and have read it every day since. It's made me a better person than I would have been otherwise. I want you to have it."

Kathy drew back with a surprised look on her face. "This is something special of yours."

"I've got it memorized. Besides, I've talked it over with Evelyn, and she wants me to hand it off to you."

Kathy put the paper in her pocket. "I'll take it home and make a copy, and bring back the original tomorrow."

"No, I want you to have the original. It's mine and Evelyn's gift to you."

Jerry reached out and grabbed hold of Kathy's hand. "I'm sharing this because time is short, and you need to know. If everything works out, perhaps I'll be asked to be your helper."

"I'd be thrilled."

They talked for a few more minutes, and then Kathy left the room around seven o'clock.

At nine-thirty Thursday morning, Kathy pulled into her parking space. Before heading into work, she sat thinking about the poem she had read and reread the night before. She felt its tug on her emotions and perspective of living and life. She had made a copy, and would give Jerry back the original.

Kathy arrived at the hospice wing around nine-fifty, and saw her nightshift counterpart Mary filling out paperwork at the reception desk.

Mary glanced up. "Later this morning, we're getting a new arrival named Bob Brown. He used to play professional football for one of those West Coast teams. Can you believe this, the guy is just fifty-eight, and suffering from late-stage renal failure. They don't think he'll last more than two weeks. Some of his old football buddies are expected to stop by later today. You never know."

Kathy shook her head, and then asked, "Did we lose anyone last night?"

"At twelve-thirty I walked past our friend Jerry's room and he seemed to be talking to someone—maybe his imaginary Evelyn again. I noticed a slight glow in the room, and assumed he had left the TV on. A little later, I stopped in to check his vitals. He was lying on his back in his pale-yellow pajamas deceased. His window was open and I remember it being closed earlier. A red rose lay on the chair next to his bed." She pointed. "I put the rose in that vase. It looks so beautiful. Why don't you take it home with you?"

Mary got up to leave. "Anyway, they picked up his body an hour ago. And that's about it."

# STORY THREE

## Friday with Tom

"You want another?" Tom asked.

Slumped at the end of the bar, Jack glanced over. "Bring it on."

"This one's on the house."

"Thanks."

Tom handed the beer to Jack. "I hear they let the fucker out a couple of weeks ago."

Jack grabbed the fifteen-ounce mug. "You heard right. I ran into him on Grand Avenue yesterday. He talked trash and flashed a pistol as I walked by. He's back at his old corner."

Tom Murphy, short and pudgy around the middle, leaned across the bar. "The son-of-a-bitch should have been executed, or at least put away for life. This damn state doesn't care about people like me or you. The guy that killed Bobbie Kennedy has been in prison for over fifty years, and he ain't ever getting out. What's it been, four years since that bastard murdered your brother?"

In a slurred voice, Jack said, "It happened on Phil's sixteenth birthday."

Tall, lanky, with curly brown hair and a couple days growth of beard, Jack Chase grew up in this neighborhood. At thirty-two, with his brother dead, he was alone. The rest of his family lay buried at Holy Cross Cemetery.

Tom gripped the bar with both hands. "I know what I'd do. And I wouldn't worry about the consequences."

"Something will be done," Jack said.

"I've got a .45 under the counter—just ask."

Jack nodded. "I need to think about it, but that might be the solution."

Tom wrapped his plump fingers around a cigarette. "Twenty years ago we'd cram a hundred and fifty folks in here every Friday and Saturday night. Guys brought their wives and girlfriends. Men with calluses in dirty, sweaty work clothes crowded at the bar smoking and drinking. We had fights, but never with knives or guns. The place hummed with all those factory jobs around here. Pat McGovern opened Paddy's in 1935, now one of his grandkids owns it. She lives in Florida and been trying to sell the building for years. No takers for this dead neighborhood."

Tom's attention was drawn to a panhandler hustling customers for the price of a drink. He marched over and without saying a word grabbed the guy's long scruffy hair and ran him out.

Face flushed and out of breath, Tom sat on a stool next to Jack. "That guy's father was a good man. Who knew his son would turn out a piece of trash." Tom kept his eye on the door. "I took social security at sixty-two. It ain't much, but it keeps me from starving. I'd never fucking beg."

Tom glanced around the room. "It's eight o'clock on a Friday night, and we got maybe fifteen people here. Some folks come in to get out of the cold, or use the toilet. I throw everybody out at eleven o'clock and close up the place. A couple months back I checked the restroom and found a young guy plopped on the toilet seat unconscious, a needle in his arm. The son-of-a-bitch died by the time the paramedics arrived. It used to be cigarette butts and beer cans lying all around, now its drug shit. Hell, the city provides free needles to dopers. What next—free dope? This fucking world is upside down."

Tom lit a cigarette. "I haven't seen you in a while. Where have you been?"

Jack slid off the bar stool. "Here and there, I got a job as a welder. I put in a lot of overtime hours to make ends meet, so it keeps me busy. I live in an apartment about thirty minutes from here."

As Jack headed toward the restroom, he said, "By the way, I'm getting married."

When Jack returned, Tom grabbed him by the arm. "What's this business about getting married?"

"Great gal, I met her about six months ago. She's from a small town, a real country girl. We'll stop by—you'll like her. Her name is Carrie Shannon."

"What a good Irish name, you can't go wrong there. I'd love to meet her."

An hour passed as a handful of older folks, stuck in the neighborhood like Tom, drifted in and out.

Jack studied the room. The oak floor was cracked and crusty, smelling of spilled beer fermenting in the floorboards; blotches of gray paint hung loose from the walls; several overhead lights were out leaving parts of the room in shadows, and the wooden tables and chairs were worn and rickety. The restroom had stunk, and the basin water took a long time to go down. While drying his hands on a paper towel, Jack smashed a large black spider climbing up the wall. He'd be afraid to sit down in there. The place looked and smelled like the neighborhood.

At eleven o'clock, Tom locked up the place and strolled to Jack's newer model silver Jeep, the lone vehicle in the parking lot. The temperature had dipped into the low fifties, normal for Gulf City in late October.

As they leaned against the car, Tom said, "It's good to see you. I remember when your pop and his dad would come in almost every Friday night after getting off work at that assembly plant. Nice guys with a lot of great stories. It hurt when that plant closed. That was the nail in the coffin."

Jack nodded. "I thought I might work there one day. Those businesses are overseas making even more money for their billionaire owners."

Tom laughed as a rodent scurried across the parking lot. "See how skinny that rat is. Even he can't make a decent living around here."

Tom told how a derelict got stabbed to death fighting over a half-bag of cheese puffs on the pub's parking lot, and mentioned an old friend of Jack's father had passed. Two young men walking past the pub stopped and stared. They moved on after Tom opened his jacket exposing the .45 in his waistband.

At the sound of a wailing dog, Tom said, "I'll bet he wants out of here."

Jack agreed, and then offered Tom a ride home.

Tom headed across the parking lot. "It's only a few blocks." He pointed to his weapon. "It's available whenever you need it."

"I've got a marriage coming up, so I have some tough decisions to weigh. I've taken next week off to decide. You'll hear from me."

## Sunday with Carrie

After Sunday services at Calvary Baptist church, Carrie and Jack headed over to Mom's Place, a small diner planted in the middle of the arts community on the East side of town. It overlooked the river; you could watch tugs and other craft float by as you drank coffee and munched on blueberry muffins. Located on Cherry Boulevard, a narrow street jammed with antique and craft stores, Mom's was always busy—especially on Sundays.

Jack parked on a tree-lined side street about a block from Mom's. The temperature on the dashboard read 48 degrees. A slight breeze made it feel a little cooler. Carrie wore a thick green sweater with her jeans and white tennis shoes. A blue stocking cap held down her bright-red hair. Jack, also in jeans, had on his light-gray jacket. He stood a head taller than Carrie as they strolled down the sidewalk taking in the bacon and pancake smells flowing from Mom's busy kitchen. Jack held the white-wooden door as they entered around eight-thirty.

Mom's diner had been around for fifty years. It opened at eight o'clock and closed at nine in the evening, seven days a week. It seated about one hundred. A thick dark-blue carpet cushioned the floor, while pictures of past presidents hung from the light-tan walls. The recessed lighting brightened the room. The menu was basic, and prices reasonable. The meatloaf and mash potatoes soaked in thick mushroom gravy were dinner favorites.

Half the twenty-five wooden tables, covered with white table clothes, were already filled. The line was growing fast as Mabel, their server, escorted Jack and Carrie to the last window table available. They ordered eggs, bacon, and orange juice, to be followed by coffee and pecan pie.

After the server left, Jack held Carrie's hand and gazed at her bright green eyes and dazzling smile. Fair-skinned with flowing red hair draped over her shoulders, Carrie recently turned twenty-five. She was trim, and looked great in jeans. After high school, she left her small town and served three years in the Army. She then headed to Gulf City doing basic office and clerical work when she met Jack in a country bar about six months earlier. Carrie rented a small apartment less than a mile from where Jack lived.

Carrie flashed her ring. "We've been engaged one month."

Jack nodded. "That's the smartest thing I've ever done. And I'll never do anything that smart again."

The sun poked through the clouds and brightened up what had been an overcast day. Jack watched a blue sailboat navigate its way around the river's heavy barge traffic. Carrie glanced at the growing crowd on Cherry Street as customers mulled around waiting for the antique stores to open at nine o'clock. Mom's, now packed and noisy, had a line trailing out the door.

Mable arrived with their order. "Let me know when you're ready for your coffee and pie."

After Mable left, Carrie said, "Let's do a church wedding."

"We can forget about my old church Saint Michael's. It closed about five years ago."

"First Baptist will do. I know the pastor, and am sure we can get a date set within the next few months."

"That sounds good to me. Later we'll throw a reception at a restaurant where you can meet some of my old friends. There's a guy named Tom I want you to get to know. He was close with my dad and grandfather, and could share great stories with you."

"I'd love to meet all your friends."

Jack grinned. "Not all of them."

Carrie thought a moment. "What do you think about Sarafina's? They got great Italian food, and I know Kerry the manager. She could get us the big room in the back on short notice."

"Call Kerry and we'll get this done before Christmas. We'll put up our first Christmas tree together."

Jack signaled for their coffee and pie, and then glanced out the window. "I wish my brother Phil could be at our wedding."

"I'm so sorry about your brother. I would have loved to have met him. From what you told me, he sounded like such a nice guy."

Jack glanced away from Carrie. "Damn, I miss him."

Carrie gestured toward an older couple with a couple of small children seated across from them. "How well behaved, they got to be their grandkids. It must be nice."

Jack nodded, and then signaled for the check.

They decided to drive past the home where Jack grew up, and then explore a nature preserve forty highway minutes from the city. As they headed toward the car, a dog's bark caused Carrie to dart into the street and scoop up a small white poodle just as a car slammed on its brakes. Back on the sidewalk, she hugged the animal, kissed its forehead, and then angrily searched for its owner.

A heavyset, middle-aged woman in gray sweatpants and lavender sweater waved from across the street, and then approached Carrie. "That's my Bootsie, she loves to run."

Before handing the dog over, Carrie said, "Where's its leash? It could have been killed."

The woman grabbed the dog and walked away.

Jack put his arm around Carrie. "She didn't even thank you."

Twenty-five minutes later, Jack showed Carrie homes of long-ago friends on Grand Avenue, and empty buildings, some burnt out, where he and his parents shopped.

Jack swung onto Harper Street; about halfway he stopped and pointed to a two-story brick flat. "That's where we lived, my dad's parents on the first floor, and me, Mom and Dad, and little Phil on the upper floor. Each floor had a kitchen and two rooms. It was a struggle, but they made it work. There was elegance in that."

"Why is there a vacant lot in the middle of all those buildings?" Carrie asked.

"The Zmijewskis lived there. Mom and Dad, plus eight kids crammed in that flat. Andy and his twin brother Tom were my best friends. We played ball, did our First Communion together, and rode our bikes around the neighborhood and a park nearby. God, we had a lot of fun. I ain't heard from them in years. They could be dead as far as I know."

Carrie reached for the door handle, and Jack said, "We aren't getting out."

He slapped the dashboard. "Look at all the stinking trash, broken bricks, and pieces of glass. No self-respecting fly or cockroach would live around here."

Jack headed West on Hwy. 70 to the Carnegie Wildlife Center, a thirty-thousand acre wilderness preserve forty miles from Gulf City. Carrie loved the woods and country. However, this would be a new experience for Jack, a city boy.

Jack parked near a pavilion. Five minutes later he and Carrie were hiking a nature trail splattered with fall bursts of red, yellow, orange, and green strung high from thick maple, birch, and oak trees. Bulky viburnums, azaleas, and chokeberry shrubs ringed the walking path stacked with discarded leaves and branches. Temperatures, pushed by a soft breeze, had climbed to the mid-fifties. An earthy mix of rich evergreen and woodsy decay scented the mild air.

They dodged snakes, ran across slow-moving box turtles, bushy-tailed rabbits, and purple butterflies. Overhead chatter from blue birds, robins, and cardinals accompanied Jack and Carrie as they cleared back bush and tree branches along the leaf-covered dirt path. Jack stopped to watch a small gray squirrel scamper up an oak tree, clutching something in its teeth.

After a couple of miles, they settled on a rotting log overlooking a wide stream. Fast-moving water slapped the rocks and echoed up the creek bank as the current swept dead leaves and branches downstream. The late day sun wrapped everything with a warm glow.

Jack brushed away a bright-red leaf clung to Carrie's green sweater, and then put his arm around her. "I've been thinking about the little gray squirrel I saw a while back. After a few weeks, he's on his own. He's got to find something to eat or he starves. Or a hawk finds him, and it ends that way. It's a tough neighborhood for the folks living here. No welfare, health care, or retirement plan when you get old. It's a struggle to survive, and fairness has nothing to do with outcomes. Free and fair don't exist and the folks here know it."

Jack kissed Carrie, and said, "You have to take care of your own business. Some decisions work out well and some don't. We all live or die with them—like that squirrel."

Carrie squeezed Jack's hand. "Getting away from the city can help you think. After we're married, let's spend more time here. It has solitude and warmth you can't find in brick and mortar."

Jack nodded as he tossed a rock in the creek. "This place does grow on you."

The wind picked up, bending branches and loosening a sky full of colorful leaves. Carrie pointed toward a small thin deer as it approached the creek and bent down to drink. The crack of a falling tree branch spooked the animal and it fled up the forested hillside and disappeared into a patch of maple trees.

Jack rubbed Carrie's shoulder. "I hope that deer and squirrel make the right decisions."

On the way back, they passed a couple dressed in matching green safari outfits, with wide-brim yellow bush hats, and black boots. Jack guessed they were somewhere in their sixties. Accompanying them was a tan terrier exploring the woods at the end of a long leash. They exchanged hellos, and continued on.

Carrie nudged Jack. "Maybe that's us in thirty years."

Jack shook his head as he kicked a pile of leaves. "Let's agree never to wear matching "Jungle Jim" outfits."

Carrie laughed. "That's fair enough."

When they arrived at the car Carrie noticed a black-and-white kitten scrounging though a discarded fast-food container nearby. She ran over and picked him up.

Carrie cradled the cat. "He's skin and bones. I'm taking him home with me."

Jack started up the engine. "It's his lucky day. If we hadn't come along—who knows."

Carrie stroked the animal. "We'll name him Eli."

"Welcome to your new family, Eli."

## Monday at Saint Michael's

Jack rose around nine-thirty, put on the coffee, and texted Carrie. He mentioned he planned to take a drive past his old grade school. She said things were fine, Eli loved canned food and his new home, and someday she would like to see that grade school.

Jack grabbed his light jacket, lit a cigarette, and headed out the door. Saint Michael's lay across town, about a thirty-five minute drive with all the stoplights.

Established in 1902, tall and stately Saint Michael's took five years to complete. For generations its bell had sounded on the hour throughout the surrounding Irish, German, and Polish communities. The church and school had been the neighborhood's center of religious, social, and cultural life. In the early 1960s the church had two thousand active families. Classrooms overflowed with students taught math, science, and the Catholic Way by tough Franciscan nuns not afraid to smack the back of a kid's head. The student population had dwindled to two hundred when Jack graduated and shrunk to seventy-five when Phil finished the eighth grade. It had been five years, after carting off statutes of saints and vessels of Holy Water, since the Bishop had ordered the place shuttered.

Jack pulled over to the curb and examined the worn brown-brick buildings. A few windows were broken; gang signs spray painted here and there, and lots of scraggly weeds poking through cracks in the asphalt. He expected worse.

Hunched over the metal bench near the school's entrance was an old man in black pants and gray sweater. Jack approached the guy, not sure whether he was sick or a neighborhood tramp getting over an "all-nighter."

Jack noticed the man clutching a rosary. "Are you OK?"

The old man raised his head, and stared a moment. "Aren't you Jack Chase?"

Jack reached out his hand. "Father Dempsey, how are you, sir? I haven't seen you since my brother's funeral."

Jack gazed at the old priest. "My brother and I had great times here, and learned a lot in eight years."

"Most of my life as a priest was at Saint Michael's. I retired a year before the Bishop closed things up. It's a shame, and it hurts. I come back to reminisce about the great students and teachers, the Friday fries the Christmas and Easter celebrations, school picnics and pageants. I think of all the blessed souls that made the parish such a special place in those days."

Jack nodded. "With all due respect, sermons and prayers didn't save this neighborhood and aren't going to resurrect broken buildings and lives. All that's left is back-in-the day memories ... and they die with us."

Jack's attention was drawn to musical sounds from a Mister Softy ice-cream truck.

Jack waved as the truck approached. "I can't believe that truck still works this damn neighborhood. Be back in a minute, Father."

Jack ordered chocolate and strawberry shakes, and cautioned the driver to be careful. The young Asian pointed to a pistol in the truck.

Jack handed Father Dempsey a shake. "You always liked chocolate."

Father Dempsey laughed. "Oh, my, I haven't had one of these since a school picnic. Thanks so much. I remember when you decided not to enter the Seminary. God and I almost had you."

"That wasn't your fault. Let's say, God felt the Marines were a better fit."

They talked about Jack's dad and grandfather, both long-time active parishioners.

Father Dempsey said, "Your dad was so handy, he could fix anything. He saved Saint Michael's a lot of money. Your grandpa, in that brown suit, ushered every seven o'clock Sunday mass for twenty years straight. And your mom and grandma made the best cakes for the bake sales."

Jack asked about his favorite teacher Sister May, and learned she had died six months earlier in a car accident.

When Father Dempsey mentioned Phil, Jack stood, and said, "The lousy punk that murdered my little brother is out already. My brother's life isn't worth much to our so-called justice system."

Father Dempsey put his hand on Jack's shoulder. "Leave it to the judgement of God."

Jack raised his voice. "We can't kick justice into Eternity and hope for the best."

Jack paused, and gazed at the aged priest. "Sorry, Father, you hit a topic that sets me off. I don't mean to take it out on you. I'm staring at that problem right now."

"Don't hesitate to call me at the retirement center whenever you want to talk about anything."

Jack agreed, and then changed the subject.

Father pointed toward a large oak tree. "Remember all the cardinals and robins that nested up there. I stopped by here last spring and didn't see or hear anything moving around."

Jack noticed, among the layers of wrinkles, a three-inch scar above the priest's right eye. "When did you pick that up? Did you fall or bump into something?"

The priest shook his head. "Right here, a couple summers ago a young kid tried to rob me. He bounced a brick off my forehead when he found out I didn't have any money. I pray for him every day."

"You're lucky the punk didn't have a gun. I'll bet he has one now—if he's still alive."

Jack slow walked the old priest back to his car, and got his telephone number. After they parted, Jack sent Carrie a text message to be sure to include a place for Father Dempsey at the wedding reception.

## Tuesday evening with Carrie and Eli

Jack stopped by Carrie's tight one-bedroom apartment at seven o'clock. They planned to discuss the invite list for the wedding and watch some television. Jack brought a bottle of merlot to go with the spaghetti Carrie had made. They set the plates and glasses on a small folding table next to the kitchen. Carrie opened a can of soft cat food for Eli.

Jack watched skinny Eli devour the food. "He's lucky you came along, and so am I. For fun, let's mail him an invite to the reception."

"Of course, and we'll understand why he can't come due to prior commitments."

Jack poured the wine, and said, "I've got the two bedrooms, and larger kitchen. We'll start at my apartment, but I'd like to find a ranch home with a nice fenced yard. Maybe we add a swing set in the back."

Carrie smiled. "What a great plan, I'm holding you to it."

"We can start moving your stuff over to my place as soon as you'd like."

After dinner, they flipped on the TV and relaxed on the couch.

Carrie put on Chanel 30. "They're showing *Dead Reckoning* followed by *The Big Sleep*, two of my favorite Bogart movies."

Jack scooted closer to Carrie. "Bogie faced challenges head on. You ate a bullet if you wronged him. He was cool."

Little Eli joined—playing and jumping between them. After adding and dropping a couple of names, they finally narrowed the wedding invite list to about twenty-five friends and family. Jack spent the night, leaving when Carrie headed off to work the next morning.

## Wednesday's visit with Smoke

Jack knew Smoke—real name James Gordon—from high school days. They played pickup basketball in the schoolyard, and had become friends before Smoke got expelled in the tenth grade for beating up the gym coach. Later, Smoke got involved in burglaries, robberies, and some drug dealing. He served five years for assault with a deadly weapon. Smoke knew the streets, and Jack wanted his thoughts on how best to deal with the guy that killed his brother. They agreed to meet at seven-thirty at Paddy's Pub.

Smoke, at six-foot two, muscular, with braided hair, was leaning on the hood of his late-model dark-blue Mercedes when Jack arrived. They shook hands, talked for a few minutes, and then went inside.

Smoke slung his tan leather jacket over a chair in the back, while Jack picked up a couple of beers at the bar.

Tom filled the two mugs, and then leaned toward Jack. "What are you doing with that son-of-a-bitch? He's done time. He's trouble."

"I know him from way back. We're not rekindling an old friendship, but I want to discuss a few things with him."

"Be careful!"

"That's what it's all about."

Jack handed Smoke a beer, and sat down.

Smoke glanced at the empty tables. "I get a call after all these years. What's up?"

Jack hesitated, and then said, "A guy needs taking care of, and I'm thinking of doing it."

"You mean killing?"

"Yes."

"Are you talking about the son-of-a-bitch who murdered Phil?"

Jack nodded. "He got released a couple of weeks ago."

Smoke shoved the beer aside and pulled a silver flask from his shirt pocket. "If he had murdered my brother, he would have been dead within twenty-four hours. You can't allow yourself to be disrespected. If you do, you look weak and the streets lose respect for you. And then you're finished."

Jack's phone rang—it was Carrie. He let it go to message, and then turned it off.

Smoke took a drink, and said, "How many men have you shot or killed?"

Jack shrugged. "None."

Smoke grinned. "The good news is getting away with killing this guy is the easy part  Cops don't regularly patrol this part of town anymore. The 911 calls have to be about a body found, or at least shots fired before you hear the sirens or see the red lights flashing."

Jack interrupted. "The homicide folks will investigate. I'll be a suspect because of my motive. I've got some pretty important plans coming up. I'd hate to spend the rest of my life worrying or facing a long prison term."

Smoke waved his hand dismissively. "A lot of folks want him dead. You wouldn't even make a top-ten list of suspects. First, the cops will celebrate this guy's death. Sure, they'll ask a few questions to fill out their paperwork. As long as you aren't standing over the body with a smoking gun when the cops roll up, you won't have trouble getting away with killing a punk like that."

"What about his friends wanting revenge?"

"He doesn't have friends, just a lot of enemies."

Jack picked up his empty mug. "You want something?"

Smoke held up his flask. "I'm good."

Tom refilled Jack's mug. "Are you OK? It seems intense over there."

"I've got a decision to make."

Smoke lit a long thin cigar, and propped his right leg on one of the chairs. "Let's discuss the tough part of this. Can you pump bullets into a dude until he's dead? Not everybody's up for that kind of action. The first shots can be a few feet away, but the last ones have to be done standing over him. You want to make sure he can't rise like Lazarus."

Jack shrugged. "I won't know until I'm facing him."

"That won't do. You have to know whether you can pull the trigger, or forget about it. You got to have cold blood in you, or hire it done. I know people who would do it for less than a hundred dollars."

Smoke stretched his arms. "I owe you a few favors. Let me take care of this. I'll make sure it's done right. I have a beef with the guy anyway."

Jack shook his head. "You don't owe me that much. Besides, this is something I got to do myself, or not do at all."

"OK, then let me share a few things. Use a .45, or at least a 9mm. It will bring him down quick and keep him there. Also, do it when he's alone. Witnesses aren't likely to come forward around here, but you can never tell if the cops squeeze them on something else, or they have something personal against you."

Jack's and Smoke's attention was drawn to a shouting and shoving match between two bald fat old men. After a chair got knocked over, Tom approached and ordered them to quiet down or leave.

Jack laughed. "My dad worked with those guys—they're brothers. They've been brawling for as long as I've known them."

Smoke puffed on his cigar. "I know places where a stare or words lead to gunfire, even between brothers. But let's get to your problem. The dude's back selling dope on his old corner at Grand and Olive. There aren't any overhead cameras around, so that would be a good place to hit him. He works alone and gets there around eight o'clock. It's dark by then."

"How do you know all that?"

"It's my business."

Smoke snuffed out his cigar. "Park close, and wear all black clothing with a hoodie covering your face. Wait till there ain't any customers around, and then come out blasting. He carries a Glock, so don't give him a chance to pull it. Stop shooting when you're sure he's dead—remember the head shot."

Smoke leaned back in his chair. "It should be over in ten seconds. Walk away like you ain't got a care in the world. Toss the gun as fast as you can. I always use the river, and none have ever been retrieved. If the cops pick you up for whatever reason—tell them nothing. You've seen those cop shows on TV where they get the guy in a room and he starts talking. The next thing you know the dumb ass talks his way into prison. Never confess to anything."

Smoke grinned. "Most folks don't have the balls for this kind of action. Even if they kill the guy, their minds get fucked-up thinking about all that splattered blood and guts. They start to second guess their decision. They confess to their wives, girlfriends, a priest, and worse—maybe a cop. If you can't handle the back end, walk away and learn to live with it. Maybe you should wait. In his line of business he'll catch a bullet sooner or later."

Smoke checked his watch, and then slid on his jacket. "Whether it's man or beast, everybody wants and fights for the same thing."

"What's that?"

"Survival, even if it's for one more fucking day."

Jack walked out with him.

Smoke turned when they reached his Mercedes. "The street has its rules. Justice is swift, but it's as fair as a system that lets a bum out after killing your brother. You put justice into someone else's hands and they'll let you down every time."

Smoke made a call, yelled at someone, and then said, "If you start something, finish it. Never leave a job half-done. You may not get a second chance." He then sped off as Jack headed back into Paddy's.

Jack took a seat at the end of the bar, and signaled Tom for another beer.

When Tom arrived, Jack whispered, "I might need to borrow your .45. I'll let you know in a day or two."

Tom replied, "It's here whenever you need it."

Jack nodded as he turned his phone back on and saw Carrie had left four messages.

On his drive home Jack called Carrie.

Carrie sounded out of breath. "You had me worried. I thought something happened, maybe an accident."

"I'm fine. I stopped by Paddy's and drank a few beers. I met an old acquaintance and lost track of the time. It's a noisy place, so I waited till he left to call you back."

"Have I met him? Did you invite him to the wedding?"

"The wedding didn't come up, and you never met him. I haven't seen him in years. We discussed a few things, and I don't expect to hear from him again. Our paths don't cross these days."

"Well, as long as you're OK."

"I'm good. I'll call you tomorrow."

## Thursday Coffee and Sweet Rolls with Carrie

When Jack arrived at Carrie's apartment around seven-fifteen, she insisted she had to have a large slice of cheesecake with strawberries, topped with thick whipped cream. She threw on a gray sweatshirt, chased Eli away from the door, and then locked it. From her front steps, she pointed in the direction of a popular diner known as The Sweet Factory. Open from six o'clock in the morning till nine o'clock at night, it brewed strong coffees to go with tasty desserts. Located at the corner of Lexington and Broadway, the diner attracted people with a need for anything soft and sweet.

    Carrie slid her left arm around Jack's waist as they strolled down the tree-lined street. A lamp post every thirty feet and storefronts flooded the busy sidewalk with protective night-light.

    Carrie waved at a young couple across the street. "They got married a couple of months ago and are moving to California, somewhere near Los Angeles. I met them when I first moved in. Cathy and I used to spend a lot of Saturday afternoons shopping together. They're going to have a baby. I'll miss them."

    Carrie tossed a couple of dollars into a bucket in front of a bearded street musician strumming a guitar. A minute later, Jack held the glass door as they entered the diner. The tiled floor was a butterscotch tan. To the left a cashier and small bar area served "to go" orders. Seating consisted of small wooden tables, four chairs to a table.

    Carrie led Jack to window seat facing Lexington Avenue. "I stop by here a lot of mornings before work. I get coffee with a couple of sugar-coated jelly donuts and people watch through this big glass window. I notice folks in a rush, while others stroll past gabbing on a cellphone. Most mornings a skinny beggar works this corner. Boy, he smells bad. And then there's this well-dressed old guy from the neighborhood who lives by himself and always seems irritated. I've waved and said hi a couple of times when we pass on the street, yet he ignores me. He's vexed about something, maybe a lot of things. He can't be happy."

"Vexed has always been with us. Cain was vexed and took it out on Abel. It happens in the best of families."

"Not with us—never with us."

Carrie ordered cheesecake with a double serving of strawberries topped with a scoop of thick whipped cream, and a large coffee. Jack got the lemon sweet roll.

After the server left, Jack said, "I wonder when the ill wind that crushed the other side of town will get here. The bad boys always show up sooner or later, and they'll win."

"We got a neighborhood watch, and the police patrol all the time."

"That didn't save my old neighborhood, and it won't save this quaint little diner."

Jack raised his voice. "I'm getting you out of here before anything happens. As soon as we're married, we'll start looking for a place outside of the city. Maybe we move to the suburbs or further out. I want you safe from those thugs out there. You know what they did to my brother."

The food arrived, and the conversation moved from sports, to work, to reexamining the invite list for their wedding reception. They agreed to purchase a pair of lamps Carrie spotted at an antique store.

Carrie touched Jack's hand as he gazed out the window. "The past few weeks you seem a little distracted and upset. Is it the marriage?"

"Being with you is the most important thing in my life. That won't ever change. But life produces challenges we have to face."

"Please share! Whatever it is, we'll face together."

"Don't worry, everything will be fine. We'll get those lamps this weekend."

As they rose to leave, Carrie said, "We'll name our first son Phil."

"He'd like that."

On the walk back an old drunk flipped an empty whiskey bottle in the air that broke at Carrie's feet. Jack tossed the guy to the ground and twisted his arm until he apologized. Carrie intervened as Jack continued to curse and pound the guy. The drunk limped off clutching his side.

When they reached Carrie's apartment, she said, "Everybody calls him Binky. He's a harmless old man with a drinking problem. I pity him."

Jack kissed Carrie, and said, "It's become too easy to tolerate bad behavior, that's how neighborhoods begin their descent. Guys like that are due an occasional ass kicking. It makes them think twice the next time."

"He's not doing much thinking these days."

"That falls on him—bums are self-made."

Jack turned as he descended the steps. "We're getting out of this damn city."

## Friday's visit to Holy Cross Cemetery

Jack rose at seven o'clock, and sent Carrie a text. She responded she was fine, and heading off to work. He grabbed his coffee, lit a cigarette, and plopped on the beige-colored cotton sofa. He planned to drive over to Holy Cross. He didn't like going to the cemetery, and hadn't been there since Phil was laid to rest next to his mom and dad. But some things had to be said in person.

Temperatures had dipped into the low forties. Jack showered and shaved, combed his short brown hair, and headed to his car in jeans and dark-blue navy peacoat. He stopped by Patties' Flower Shop and picked up a dozen red roses for his mom and grandma.

Jack passed several crowded graveside services as he drove the cemetery's long narrow road to the family's leaf-strewn plot. Near a maple tree lay three generations under five cold stones. Jack ran his hand over the headstones as he recalled Grandma buying him his first comic book, Mom packing his lunch in a brown-paper bag and walking him to school in the early grades at Saint Michael's, Dad helping him with homework and building model airplanes, Grandpa taking him to baseball games, and the family heading every Sunday morning to church for seven o'clock mass. All that love, laughter, sacrifice, and fun packed in those yesterdays. He figured they would be rolling over in those graves if they knew what became of their working-class neighborhood. Jack shared the news about Carrie knowing they would be happy with his choice.

And then there was Phil . . . thin, short blond hair, always smiling. His was a gentle life not given its chance to love, marry, or have a family. Jack remembered the plea deal where the prosecutor agreed to call a robbery ending in a bullet to the back of the head involuntary manslaughter. A six-year sentence, and out in four.

Jack placed a red rose on Phil's gravestone. "No matter what else happens that bastard will live long enough to regret killing you. Everybody must pay their bills, and it's his turn. That's justice; they haven't given me any other choice."

Jack drove around for a few hours, grabbed a quick lunch, and sent a text to Carrie. He arrived at Paddy's a little before five o'clock.

Jack leaned across the bar and whispered. "Tom, I need to borrow your .45."

Tom wrapped the weapon in a towel and handed it to Jack.

Jack shoved the gun in his waistband. "Do you want it back?"

"Hell no, I'll report it stolen."

"Report it stolen by tomorrow, the next day at the latest."

"I understand."

Jack turned as he left. "Thanks partner."

Jack slid the gun under the front seat, and scouted his target's hangout searching for the best place to park and approach. Around eight o'clock he spotted the bastard at his corner spot waving his gun at someone, and then shoving it back inside his bright-blue windbreaker. On the way home Jack bought a black sweatshirt with hoodie, black pants, and a pair of black leather gloves. He figured tomorrow night.

## Saturday's Rendezvous

Jack phoned Carrie around ten o'clock in the morning and broke their date for later that day. He explained something work related would tie him up till well into the night. He promised to call as soon as the job was finished.

After a bacon and scrambled egg breakfast, Jack stretched out on the couch and flipped on his favorite cable channel. He had found a place to park, and if everything went right the bastard would be dead by ten-thirty that night, eleven o'clock at the latest. He planned to head out around nine that evening. The .45 lay on the small wooden coffee table ready to go. Over the next three hours, Jack went through a half-pack of cigarettes and a couple of beers.

At the conclusion of *This Gun for Hire*, his favorite Alan Ladd movie, Jack flipped off the TV, picked up the gun, and thought about what lay ahead. The plan was simple. Walk up to his target and continue shooting till the bastard was dead. And get it done within Smoke's timetable. What could go wrong? He thought about it, and then glanced over at the framed photo of Carrie on the side table. He realized a lot could go wrong. His first shots might miss and he could end up being the homicide victim. Although unlikely, witnesses could be a possibility. And what if the bastard survived, then he would be the hunted. That might put Carrie in harm's way. That was unacceptable, so either he or the bastard would die—maybe both.

Jack grabbed a pen and note pad, and began a letter explaining his actions. He wrote about Phil and justice—not revenge. And other things like how the legal system failed his brother, the destruction of his neighborhood, the closing of the church he grew up in, and the indifference to it all. Somehow it all tied together and killing this punk was a strike back at all that. He hoped some good would come of it even if he didn't survive. He closed by asking Carrie's to understand he had to do this.

Jack folded the sheet of paper and placed it inside a white envelope. After writing TO CARRIE on the back of the envelope, he set it next to her photo. If he didn't make it back, Carrie had a key to his apartment and would find it. Jack wondered about his and Carrie's future. He thought of praying, but decided not to drag God into this.

Jack lay on the sofa till eight-thirty when he changed into his all-black outfit. He paced around the apartment, gazed at Carrie's photo—that great smile and glowing red hair, and then checked his watch. It was nine o'clock...time to go kill a bad man.

Jack pulled out of his apartment complex for the drive across town. His weapon, with a dirty rag thrown over it, lay on the front passenger seat. Next to the weapon lay his new black leather gloves. At a stoplight a mile or so from his apartment he watched a couple of teenagers push an old woman to the ground, grab her purse, and disappear into the night. On Clark Avenue he passed Assumption parish as its church bell chimed on the half-hour. He then headed north on Grand Avenue.

At nine-fifty he spotted the son-of-a-bitch in his torn jeans and windbreaker leaning against the side of the corner building—alone. Jack hoped, if all went well, the bum had fifteen or twenty-minutes to live. The previous day Jack found an alley down the street from his target. It would keep him and his vehicle out of sight.

Jack slipped on his gloves and grabbed the gun. He scanned the narrow alley, except for broken glass, oil smells, old tires, and a couple of rusty water heaters, it was clear. The .45 felt heavy as he walked toward the goal around the corner of the empty brick building which used to be a shoe factory employing hundreds. Jack wondered what he would do if someone else showed up while he was firing—kill them too or run. And what if the piece-of-shit already had his gun out? No matter; tonight was do it or die. He recalled Smoke's ten-second rule as he got closer.

Jack crouched in the dark, his target around the corner of the building—thirty feet away. He made sure the extra-large black hoodie covered most of his face, and gripped his gun. Other than passing vehicles, it was quiet.

Jack took a deep breath, and whispered, "Time to pay up." At that moment a speeding red, late model four-door sedan pulled up to the curb in front of the building. Two men wearing yellow bandanas exited the vehicle, one from the front passenger side the other from the rear door, firing as they went. Jack counted a dozen rapid explosions and one final burst. A few seconds later the car sped off. Jack peeked around the corner and saw his target lying motionless on his back, his shirt and pants soaked red. Blood spurted from his forehead and rolled down his cheeks, his eyes and mouth frozen open with expression of shock. He was past talking or threatening.

The bastard was dead, snuffed fast and efficient by real street professionals. Smoke would be proud.

Jack shoved his gun in his belt, and lowered his hoodie. As he strolled back to his car he felt a sense of relief, and wondered if Providence had interceded to place this piece of justice into someone else's hands.

He glanced over as he drove past the corpse and noticed a couple of teenagers. One stood in a growing pool of blood clutching the dead man's gun, while the other picked through his pockets. This corner now belonged to someone else.

Jack rapped his fingers on the dashboard, and phoned Carrie. "The job is finished. If you're hungry we can head over to the Pizza Shack."

Carrie noticed an upbeat tone in Jack's voice. "I'd love to grab a pizza. I'll be waiting out front when you arrive."

Jack shoved the .45 under the front seat. He would get it back to Tom on Monday.

## STORY FOUR

Built in 1895, the home at 2800 Sycamore Street was often called the Palace.

For many years, this was the place to visit if you were, or planned to be, somebody. Mounted within its three-story, thick gray limestone walls were thirty large windows and two balconies. Six white marble pillars, imported from Italy, anchored a massive wooden arch that jutted out over twin twenty-foot oak entrance doors. Sunlight bounced off the brown clay-tiled roof casting a vibrant glow to passersby.

A walkway of deep-blue cobblestones led to the front porch, where two lamps, one on each side, flickered from seven to twelve each evening. A separate driveway steered carriages to a large stable area in the back, later converted to a six-car garage. A sturdy six-foot cast iron fence surrounded the seven acres and twenty-five thousand square-foot home. In its prime, regular guests included U.S. Presidents, famous poets, academics, and Wall Street titans.

On a warm Sunday afternoon in September 1980, a cab pulled to the curb at 2800 Sycamore Street. Out of the cab stepped ninety-three-year-old Alice Hoffmann wearing a lavender dress that ran just below her knees, white gloves, and tennis shoes. She was thin and average height, with shoulder-length gray hair. A dash of rouge perked up her pale wrinkled cheeks.

Alice gazed at the large broken down building as two young men in T-shirts and jeans approached. Joe, short and pudgy with dark hair, held a metal detector; Mike, tall and skinny with blond hair, carried a shovel and folded newspaper.

Alice swung her purse over her shoulder, and then pointed at the metal detector. "Are you boys on a treasure hunt?"

Mike held up the newspaper. "It says this place will be torn down next week, and mentions a missing coin collection. We figured we'd root around—maybe strike it rich."

In a soft voice, Alice said, "People have been looking for those coins for years. I don't know how many boards got pulled up and holes dug. But who knows, maybe you guys get lucky."

Mike shrugged. "Joe and I ain't got much to lose but a little time. Why are you here?"

"I worked in there for fifty years, and wanted a last look before the city tore it down."

"What did you do?" Joe asked.

"I cooked, cleaned, and sometimes they even let me answer the front door. I started after dropping out of high school. I was sixteen and my family needed money. I was pretty back then, and my mom hoped I'd meet a wealthy guy here and marry him. That didn't work out. Now I'm just an old bag of bones waiting to be torn down like this building. That's the way it goes. How old are you guys?"

"We're both seventeen," Mike said.

Alice smiled. "That's a fun age."

Alice learned the boys attended Cleveland Public, her old high school, and they lived near where she grew up. They agreed to explore the Palace together. Its old cast iron fence was bent, broken, or rusted—the gate gone altogether. As they walked toward the entrance the lush green lawn that Alice remembered was now splattered with ugly thistle weed, dandelions, and patches of lifeless dirt. The imposing front doors, their wood long rotted, hung open. Pigeon's flapped about the ceiling as they entered the two-story foyer.

Alice gazed upward. "They had a huge crystal chandelier that lit up like the sun. Mrs. Jefferson bragged on it forever—had it shipped from Paris. And there was a tall, at least seven foot, dark mahogany grandfather clock in here that chimed on the quarter-hour. It was lovely."

Mike dropped the newspaper on the crusty floor loaded with bird droppings. "According to the article, the people that built this were the 'fat cats' of their day."

Alice nodded. "Oh, yes, Mr. David Jefferson Sr. was one of the richest people in America. He founded the family fortune in silver mines out in Colorado, and later built a brewery. Jefferson Lager was the biggest seller in twenty states at the time of Prohibition. Money flowed in, and they liked to spend. I overheard Mrs. Jefferson say this place cost a million dollars to build. Can you imagine what it would cost today?"

Joe asked, "Where do you think we should start looking for those coins?"

Alice shrugged. "You could start outside near the old garden area. David Jefferson Jr. liked to hang out there, and he owned them at the time of their disappearance. He inherited the collection after his dad passed. When David Sr. died in 1916 they valued the coins at two-hundred thousand dollars. Mrs. Jefferson never put in an insurance claim or called the police after she said they were missing, so I don't think they were stolen."

"When did they first go missing?" Mike asked.

"Right after David Jr. committed suicide, and the creditors and IRS came calling in September 1948. By that time the family had hit hard times. Not by most peoples' standards, but a big come-down from where they were. Their breweries got closed by Prohibition, so they had already sold off those assets. Later, the silver mines began to play out and there was less coming in from there. The problem was David Jr. and his mom knew how to spend money, but never learned to make it."

Joe gripped the metal detector. "Where's this garden area?"

They walked through the house, sidestepping rotting boards, bits of broken plaster, and empty bottles of liquor. Foul odor poured from a fly-covered raccoon lying stiff in a corner of what used to be the kitchen.

Alice wiped away a tear as they emerged in a patio just outside the kitchen. She pointed to a weed-filled patch about fifty feet away, and then leaned against a partially intact red-brick wall that enclosed the patio. Joe started sweeping the weedy area with his detector, while Mike stayed back with Alice.

"When you find something, I'll come over and dig," Mike said.

Alice surveyed the patio, and then turned to Mike. "In warm weather, David Sr. used to take breakfast out here. We had to have his meal ready by seven o'clock. He'd come dressed in a blue or gray pin-stripe suit, hair combed, black shoes polished, and sit down to two scrambled eggs, four pieces of bacon, a buttered biscuit, followed by a pastry. I'd pour him three cups of strong black coffee. When I took away his empty plates, he always thanked me in his baritone voice. I never got a thank you from anyone else around here. I can still picture him with his big handlebar mustache, lighting a cigar, checking his gold pocket watch, and then heading to his downtown office—even on Saturdays. In the early days he'd be driven to work in a carriage. Later, a chauffeur drove him in one of their six cars. He was rich, but never took it for granted. On the other hand, Mrs. Jefferson always had breakfast in bed. She'd ring between nine and nine-thirty, demand this or that, and finally came downstairs around eleven o'clock."

Joe yelled, "I found something."

Mike excused himself, and started to dig. After a few hurried moments, he tossed the discovery—a rusty beer can—into the weeds. Joe continued to sweep the area as Mike dug up more worthless objects.

After ten minutes, Mike returned to the patio while Joe kept up the search.

Alice shared more stories dating back seventy plus years, impressing Mike with her insights on long-ago people, their looks, and attitudes. Her enthusiasm was contagious, and made Mike feel like he was reliving it with her.

Joe kicked the ground and shouted a couple of profanities in frustration.

Alice pointed toward broken-down foundation walls, a hundred feet from the main house. "Check over there, that's where they had the chapel."

Mike raised his eyebrows. "They had their own chapel?"

Alice nodded. "The nearest church, a little over a mile away, was Saint Jerome's. Mrs. Jefferson felt it attracted too much middle-class riff-raff. She didn't want to share a pew or be seen with them, so she insisted a chapel be built for their own personal use. They imported the stones and wooden pews from a $17^{th}$ century church due to be torn down somewhere in Italy just outside Rome. The stained-glass windows, gold candle holders, and vessels that held Holy Water came from France.

"Bishop Carlson came out and blessed the chapel, and Mrs. Jefferson named it Saint Margaret's, after her favorite saint. Mrs. Jefferson even bought relics of the saint from somebody in Scotland. The chapel seated eighty. The aged gray stone walls and interior gave the impression the chapel had rested there for hundreds of years. Mrs. Jefferson kept it locked most of the time, and held the single key. The place always smelled of incense.

"Every Sunday and all the church Holy Days, a priest from somewhere in the diocese stopped by at eleven o'clock to conduct mass for the family. Plus, whether Catholic or not, everyone who worked for them at the house also had to attend services. Of course, we had to sit in the back pew. They even had an organist come in and play church tunes. We were allowed to sing, but couldn't receive communion with the family. After mass ended, and after the Jeffersons left, the priest could distribute communion to the Catholic staff. Those were Mrs. Jefferson's rules. Bishop Carlson went along because the Jeffersons gave a lot of money to the church."

Mike shook his head. "Even then money could buy anything."

"Maybe in this life, but I doubt if money does much for you in the next. I've often wondered how well Mrs. Jefferson is faring these days—she died twenty years ago."

Alice gazed up at the cloudless afternoon sky. "That's a mystery we all solve sooner or later. I hope when I leave it's with a smile."

Joe shouted for Mike to bring his shovel. After digging a few seconds, they discovered a candlestick. Mike laughed and wondered how many prayers in this building got answered.

Alice walked over, and then pointed up at gray squirrels entering and exiting near a large second-story opening where a window used to be. "That room belonged to Mrs. Jefferson's daughter Rebecca. Spoiled rotten, but she had a sweet stroke in her. She loved to watch the gardeners' plant roses that used to surround this place. I'd be out here doing something and see her standing at the window with her short curly blond hair, sometimes dressed in her pink pajamas. She'd smile and wave down at me."

Alice hesitated, and then said, "She fell off a pony and died after striking her head on a rock. Bishop Carlson conducted the funeral mass at the chapel. She's buried at Calvary, the big Catholic cemetery. Poor kid, eight years old and it was over just like that. You never know."

After additional digging, they agreed to continue to search and explore the inside of the house.

The stink from the decaying raccoon hit them again as they entered back through the kitchen.

Mike held his nose. "Let's move on from this room."

Alice took them to a large first-floor space that used to be the billiard parlor. She shared how the gentlemen, including a U.S. President, used to drink, smoke, and make deals while shooting billiards. No women were allowed in except to serve drinks or clean, and the room always smelled of cigar smoke. Joe checked the scuffed splintered floor and graffiti covered walls with the metal detector.

Alice had already moved on to a massive room with a twenty-foot ceiling. The walls were a faded crusty green. A two-inch wide crack ran across the length of the pale-white ceiling dotted with spots of black mold. When Joe and Mike entered they looked to the right and saw Alice studying the space.

Mike asked Alice, "What did they use this for?"

Alice smiled. "This was the grand ballroom where important people danced and mingled at the Jefferson's parties. Every year they would throw a costume party a week before Halloween, another party in the spring, and then one on the Fourth of July where they hired professionals to shoot off fireworks. Caterers would take over the kitchen and set up a bar area in the dining hall which is the next room over. Made of solid oak, they had the dining table custom built to accommodate twenty-six couples.

"Mrs. Jefferson always fussed over the invite list. People came from New York, Chicago, even London and Paris. A columnist for the *Star Times* national newspaper chain used to write about the parties, and speculate why certain people got added or left off."

Alice walked to the center of the old ballroom, held her arms out, and pretended to dance. "One Fourth of July I came in with a tray to pick up empty glasses and a handsome young man asked me to dance. I was nineteen and still had my looks. I wasn't dressed nice like the rest of them, but he picked me because he wanted to be with the prettiest gal in the room. They were playing a waltz. I set down the tray, but before we got started Mrs. Jefferson intervened. She sent me back to the kitchen and told me to take the rest of the night off. Later I learned the guy who asked me to dance was a nephew of the great banker JP Morgan out of New York. I've always wondered about what might have happened if Mrs. Jefferson had left us alone. I was a good dancer."

"I'll bet you still are," Mike said.

Alice's face brightened as she signaled to a corner of the room. "That's where the orchestra would set up. The members of the band came dressed in black tuxedos and always had well-known singers as part of the entertainment. We could listen from the kitchen."

Joe interrupted. "Ma'am, is this room worth checking out?"

"This floor is solid marble. But do what you want."

While Joe scanned the walls with the metal detector, Alice strolled around nodding and whispering as if she recognized someone. Mike watched for a few moments, and then asked if this was her favorite room in the house.

Alice grabbed Mike's hand and sighed. "I really was a good dancer."

A large piece of decorative plaster broke loose from the ceiling and crashed to the floor, as they left the room.

Alice led them to the wine cellar. The steps looked a bit rickety, so she stayed at the top while Mike and Joe bypassed a few rotting boards as they descended.

Alice yelled down. "Mr. Jefferson Sr. prided himself on his wine collection. I heard him brag he had the best stocked cellar in the country. At one time he had over five hundred bottles down there. He went on wine buying trips all over the world. They always served it at his parties or whenever they had an important guest. He sure knew his wines."

The door to the cellar was gone, and a noxious odor greeted them from the dark room. Mike pulled a small flashlight from his back pocket, and he and Joe went in. Spread on the concrete floor was an assortment of cheap wine bottles, used needles, dirty blankets, and discarded plastic and fast-food paper wrappers. The rusted metal wine racks lay tipped over with some smashed. The damp smell of fresh urine hung in the air.

Joe thought he heard something crawling around, and headed toward the entrance. "I'm getting out of here."

Mike flicked off the flashlight. "I'm right behind you."

At the top of the stairs, Alice told them David Jefferson Jr. and his brother Philip spent their teenage years sneaking down there and getting drunk on Mr. Jefferson's expensive wines.

Mike glanced at Joe. "I think a dollar is the most we've ever spent on a bottle of wine."

Joe agreed, and then said, "I couldn't take the smell."

Alice waved her hand. "Don't worry, that place has been searched over. The family owed on taxes, and the coin collection was estimated to be worth over a million by the time David Jr. died. The IRS got a court order to search the place. Their agents started in the cellar and tore it apart looking. Mrs. Jefferson got forced to sell some of her jewels to settle up. She hated giving anything to anybody. After Mrs. Jefferson died, the city took the place over in 1963 for past due real estate taxes. And here it sits till next week when they smash and haul away what's left of its grand life."

The next room they entered Alice described as Mrs. Jefferson's sitting room. Its five large bay windows faced Vandeventer Avenue, and took in the afternoon sun.

Alice glanced out one of the broken windows. "Most afternoons, around three o'clock, Mrs. Jefferson would relax on a big couch near these windows and drink warm tea. Sometimes she'd have her rich cronies over, and they'd gossip for a few hours, sharing latest rumors, where they planned to vacation—most often someplace in Europe, or what new jewelry or other expensive thing they bought or planned to buy."

Alice took a deep breath, and said, "I remember during the spring and summer the pale-yellow curtains in here would sway, pushed by soft winds ushering in sweet scents from blooming beds of red, yellow, and pink roses just outside the windows. This room used to smell so good.

"The wallpaper was light-blue, the ceiling flat-white, and these oak floors were young and sturdy then. Side tables were positioned at each end of the couch, and a small wooden table in front of the couch held platters of food and pitchers of tea. There were six dark blue easy chairs lined up against the wall that we moved next to the couch whenever Mrs. Jefferson had friends over. Blue was Mrs. Jefferson' favorite color, with yellow a close second."

"Should we search in here?" Joe asked.

Alice dismissed that idea. "This was Mrs. Jefferson's sanctuary. David Jr. was in charge of the coins, and he never stepped in here."

Mike noticed four light-gray plaster casts featuring faces of small children lined next to each other, secured to the wall three feet above the remnants of a large brick fireplace. "Who are they?"

Alice rubbed the dust off the cracked and chipped figures. "Those are Mrs. Jefferson's children. She had them mounted after each birth. David Jr. was first, followed by Philip, and then the girls Rebecca and Martha. Poor little Martha was found dead in her crib at six months of age. Both girls died young, while the boys grew to manhood."

Alice stepped back and stared at the figures. "In later years, after her children had passed, Mrs. Jefferson would come in here and stare at those plaster casts for hours. God knows what went through her mind. No mother wants to live beyond her children."

"You said David Jr. killed himself. What happened to Phil?" Mike asked.

"He's presumed dead. Book-wise Phil was a lot smarter than David Jr., but had no sense in other areas. They both went to University out East. After David Jr. graduated he took a title in the family business, but didn't show up at the downtown office much. He always liked to spend and play more than work. Phil graduated a year later in 1923, and came back full of himself. David Sr., the brains, the founder, and task master, had passed back in 1916. With the girls already gone, by 1923 it was just Mrs. Jefferson and the two boys."

Joe excused himself and wandered off into another room, while Alice continued, "Phil got radicalized during his time at University, and came back embarrassed by all the advantages his family's wealth had provided. He threw names around like Lenin, Trotsky, and Stalin. Phil claimed they were building a better, fairer, more equal world. And he kept using the word Utopia. Funny thing, he never treated us house servants with any new-found respect. He had lots of arguments with his older brother and Mrs. Jefferson, stopped going to church, and started donating to radical left groups. About 1928 Phil packed his bags and headed off to that special world he wanted to be part of. You heard of it—the Soviet Union."

Mike leaned against the fireplace mantle. "What happened then?"

"I picked up the mail, and now and then letters used to arrive from over there addressed to Mrs. Jefferson. The last one arrived in 1937. Mrs. Jefferson shared it with David Jr., and I overheard her say she was very worried about Phil. Right after that letter she spent hours at the family chapel praying the rosary. The Jefferson's still had some influence, and made formal and informal inquiries. They never heard from Phil again."

Mike nodded. "I read about those times. It sounds like he got swallowed up building that perfect world. Utopia building is expensive, especially in blood and prison camps. And they end up in the same place as before, a handful of people at the top living well and making the decisions while most survive in poverty. It's chasing 'fool's gold.'"

"You know your history. I'm sure Phil has been long dead. In the end, Mrs. Jefferson accepted that. She kept his last letter for years, and then one day asked me to burn it in that fireplace over there."

Alice ran her gloved hands over the casted figures, and then headed out of the room. "A week from now they'll be broken and gone, and few—if any—will know they ever came or went."

Joe ran up swinging the metal detector. "There isn't anything on this floor. Let's head upstairs."

Mike studied the wide steps leading to the second floor. "That wooden railing looks like it's ready to fall apart. We'll take the right side and have the wall for support."

Mike glanced at Alice. "Do you want to go up there?"

Alice nodded, and then brushed her white gloved hands together to remove some of the dust. "I haven't been on that floor in almost thirty years. There was a time when I could race up those steps."

Mike and Joe placed the detector and shovel on the second floor, and then each supporting one of her arms, escorted Alice up the stairs to a long hallway that had eight rooms. Alice described them as bedrooms, some belonging to the children, and others used by guests.

Joe entered a room at the end of the hall, as Mike yelled, "Call if you find anything."

Alice poked her head inside a couple of the rooms, and turned to Mike. "I should have expected this, but the level of decay still shocks me. This place used to be so grand."

Mike hesitated, and then asked, "Do you have any children?"

Alice gazed at the floor, and then at Mike. "No children, but married briefly to a fellow named Steve Hoffmann. Chalmers is my maiden name. Steve and I met here. He was one of the gardeners. My mom hated the marriage, felt I could do a lot better. She always referred to him as that 'weed puller,' and never invited us over."

Alice glanced into another room. "It ended in less than two years. He got drafted in 1917, and sent over to fight the Germans. The Army told me he got killed some place in France, and that's where he's buried. He was a nice guy, but maybe I could have done better."

Alice fished through her purse and pulled out an old black-and-white photo of herself. "This was taken a month after I got the news of Steve's death. I was thirty and still good looking. But being a widow back then had a stigma to it, like you were unlucky or something. I never remarried."

Pounding blows and then a scream caught Mike's and Alice's attention. A few seconds later Joe came running down the hall.

"Did you find something?" Mike asked.

Joe dropped his metal detector to the floor. "The biggest damn black spider I've ever seen, slow crawling up the wall. It was at least the size of a silver dollar. I smashed it a couple times with my fist. Next thing I know a rat bolted from a hole in that wall snarling and whipping its long fleshy tail at me. I can still see its angry face. I got out of there."

"I don't blame you."

"That's the room David Jr. shot himself," Alice said.

Joe stuttered, "It felt spooky as soon as I walked in there. Maybe it's haunted."

"Why did he kill himself?" Mike asked.

Alice shrugged. "I'd say money related, but don't know. Mrs. Jefferson broke with the Catholic Church due to that. Because he was a suicide they wouldn't bury him with his father and sisters over at Calvary cemetery. Mrs. Jefferson even stopped going to her chapel. I guess the right or wrong of it is between David Jr. and God."

Mike glanced at the last set of stairs. "What's up there?"

Alice said, "The whole floor is devoted to the master suite. There was the bedroom, a large bathroom that included a huge tub and dressing room. Mr. and Mrs. Jefferson each had their own walk-in closet. The butler, who ran the household staff, told me Mr. Jefferson had fifty suits and Mrs. Jefferson had over one-hundred pairs of shoes. My husband had to borrow a suit to get married in, and I wore shoes with holes in them.

"Mr. Jefferson had his library up there, which included a lot of first edition books. A dumbwaiter led from the kitchen to their bedroom whenever Mr. or Mrs. Jefferson signaled down they wanted a late night snack or glass of wine before going to bed. I worked five years before I even got to the third floor.

"Oh, yeah, Mr. Jefferson's famous coin collection was kept there in a big safe when he was alive.

Joe said, "Let's go."

The solid oak stairs to the third floor showed wear but looked intact. However, the railing was gone. Once again, Mike and Joe escorted Alice up the steps.

Joe grabbed his metal detector, and looked at Alice. "Where was that safe?"

Alice pointed to a large hole in the wall. "It was right there. A painting used to hang in front of it."

Alice turned to Mike. "We're standing in the library room. Sliding doors separated this room from the bedroom. Mr. Jefferson Sr. loved his books. He had first editions of works from Dickens, Keats, and John Milton's *Paradise Lost*. His most prized book was Shakespeare's gathered works published in 1623, referred to as the *First Folio*. Experts valued the book collection higher than the coin collection.

Alice paused, and said, "I liked to read—still do."

"Whatever happened to those books?" Mike asked.

"He donated them to the university library where he graduated. That was in 1910. I remember Mrs. Jefferson being upset that he gave away something so valuable. She didn't care about the books, but preferred they go to auction. Mrs. Jefferson never gave anything without expecting something in return."

Joe scanned where the safe used to be, and shouted in frustration. "There isn't anything here. I'll bet those coins are long gone."

"This is a huge floor, might as well scan the rest of it while we're here. It will be our last chance," Mike said.

Alice shook her head at the torn, yellowed wallpaper, the cracks in the floor and ceiling, and the layers of dirt and dust. "Mrs. Jefferson had a big bathtub up here where she often bathed in warm milk instead of water. They'd send the heated milk up through the dumbwaiter, and from there we'd haul it over to the bathtub."

Alice examined a balcony area, window broken, missing its railings and some of its floorboards. "Sometimes, in the warm months, they used to take coffee or tea there in the evening. They owned two acres out on three sides of the house, and one acre in the front entrance. It took three landscapers working full time to keep it nice and polished for them."

Alice pointed at a discarded hot-water heater lying in the weeds, and the rusty remains of an old car. "Now it looks like a graveyard for dead or dying things. Nothing ever lasts, and maybe it's not meant to."

Joe continued a half-hearted search, while Alice shared more stories with Mike.

Near the opening for the old dumbwaiter Mike and Alice came across a large faded red spot.

Mike leaned over. "It ain't fresh, but that looks like blood."

Alice put her hand over her mouth. "Goodness, I wonder what happened."

They were staring at the spot, when Joe shouted, "I found something."

Mike grabbed the shovel and began prying a board loose where Joe had pointed. Underneath they found a wooden container the size of a shoe box.

Joe dropped to his knees, pulled out the box, and tossed off the lid.

After staring a moment, Joe reached in and held up a metal figure about six-inches long with webbed feet and all yellow except for a big red bill.

Joe handed the figure to Mike. "What's that?"

Alice rushed over. "My God, I haven't seen that in over seventy-five years. It's a toy duck Mrs. Jefferson bought for little Martha. It sat on the dresser near Martha's crib. After Martha died at six months, it disappeared. Mrs. Jefferson must have buried it there, to be near her."

Mike gave the toy to Alice. "Now it's yours."

While Alice studied the figure, a voice from below yelled, "Who the hell is up there?"

With the pounding of heavy footsteps rushing up the stairs, Alice shoved the toy figure in her purse.

Mike looked at Alice. "Is there another way out of here?"

Alice pointed at the broken dumbwaiter. "That, or jump out the balcony. It's three stories down."

Moving in front of Alice, Mike gripped the shovel with both hands, while Joe stood at his side preparing to swing the metal detector like a baseball bat.

It got quiet, and then a gravelly voice boomed, "Police, we're coming up."

A few seconds later, two husky men in police uniforms entered the room.

The officers stared at the trio, and then one asked, "How come you guys ignored the 'do-not-enter' and 'condemned' signs out front? This place is falling apart, bums and addicts hang out here, and an unsolved homicide occurred in this very room a few months back. The city is bulldozing it down next week."

The officer looked at Alice. "Ma'am, these steps and floorboards are dangerous. You could have been injured. Why are you here? Are these two your grandsons?"

Alice squeezed her purse. "I guess you could say we're on a treasure hunt. I came to rekindle old memories from when I worked here, and these two nice boys are looking for that coin collection the paper wrote about. We didn't mean any harm."

The officer responded, "It's just a pile of broken junk crawling with bugs, rodents, and bums—some dead. Ma'am, I hope you found what you were looking for, but you got to leave."

With Mike and Joe in front, the officers helped Alice down the steps. On the way down, they explained they've stepped up patrols in this high crime area, and noticed movement upstairs.

When they reached the sidewalk, Alice shook hands with the officers and promised to pray for their safety. Mike and Joe waved as the officers drove off.

Alice checked her watch. "It's five-thirty; the last bus comes at six o'clock. I'd better get down there."

Mike said, "It's getting dark, we'll walk you to the bus stop and stay till it comes."

"It's only a block."

"That's OK, we'd be glad to do it."

On the walk, Alice told them she and most of the staff got let go for financial reasons by Mrs. Jefferson in 1953. After that Mrs. Jefferson and a caretaker lived alone in that big house. The last party was in September 1945, to celebrate the end of World War II. Alice had heard Mrs. Jefferson had auctioned off her remaining jewelry and several valuable pieces of art to keep a semblance of appearances. Over the last year's most of the acreage was sold. Mrs. Jefferson passed away in 1960, at the age of eighty-four.

Alice glanced back at the house. "I read Mrs. Jefferson was found by the caretaker on Christmas Eve, slumped on her couch in the sitting room—dead."

"She died alone?" Mike asked.

"In a way, we all die alone with our last thoughts, memories, and regrets. I'm not sure it makes any difference how many folks are gathered around when you pass into Eternity."

"I never thought of death in that way, but you're right."

"At seventeen you're not meant to think of things like that. But, it's an everyday occurrence where I live now."

"Where's that?"

"Over on Goodfellow Avenue, a place called Happy Valley Retirement Home. It's a bargain basement facility that houses old folks that are broke and on Medicaid. I've been there eight years, lasted a lot longer than most. The majority of folks arrive in wheelchairs or walkers, but everybody leaves feet first. Maybe someday they'll come up with something different, but for now that's the end-game. Wealthy or poor, one day you just run out of time."

At five-fifty they arrived at the bus stop and sat on a bench inside a glass enclosure meant to keep out the rain while you waited. Headlights from oncoming cars and trucks provided the only light.

Loud car radios, screeching tires, and anxious drivers pushing car horns whistled through the night air.

Alice stretched back on the bench. "That's the most exercise I've gotten in years—it was fun. Tonight they're serving pot roast, mashed potatoes, and I think butterscotch pudding for dessert. I'll sleep like a baby."

At the approach of the bus, Mike waved to make sure it stopped.

Alice gave the boys a hug, and then wrote her telephone number on a piece of paper and handed it to Mike. "Call me, or stop by anytime. I'm always home, and I love company. Some folks never get visitors."

Mike helped Alice onto the bus, seating her right behind the driver. The bus released a cloudy burst of exhaust fumes as it pulled away. Mike and Joe watched it turn at the next corner and disappear into the night.

Joe tapped Mike on the shoulder. "Let's go. It's six blocks, and it smells like rain."

Mike nodded. "Not what I expected, but it's been quite a day. "

As they passed the old mansion, Joe said, "What a wasted afternoon. I could have watched a couple of football games on TV."

"You can do that next week, and the week after. Today's experience can never be repeated."

Joe glanced over with a surprised look. "We didn't find the coins. I met an angry nasty-assed rat. And then we got chased out by a couple of cops. Watching a football game sounds good in comparison."

"Sure, I would have liked to have found the coins. But treasure presents itself in a lot of ways. It depends on how you measure things."

"I don't know what the hell you're talking about."

"That's because you spent most of the time chasing a mysterious pot of gold instead of listening. Alice had so many interesting stories and observations. I felt her joy and frustrations from fifty years of living and working in one place. I grew up a lot this afternoon."

Joe laughed. "She's a nice old lady, but we're both still seventeen."

They walked a little further, passing a gas station where a couple of old men were pushing and shouting at each other. A police siren wailed in the distance, and Sunday evening traffic began to die down.

Mike dragged the end of the shovel over the concrete sidewalk. "In a couple of weeks I'm going to stop over to see Alice. If there's a restaurant nearby, we'll go to lunch. I think it will make her happy. Plus, she's got a lot to share. I like listening to her."

The wind picked up, and Joe felt a couple of raindrops hit his face. "We better hurry, or we'll get soaked." They started running, and disappeared down the block.

## STORY FIVE

Clinging to treetops or clumped on the ground in heaps, oak and maple leaves glowed bright red, golden yellow, shades of orange, and faded green. The temperature, nudged by a slight breeze, felt cool and comfortable. Mid-day sun cut through the forest lighting up the woods while bouncing off clear sparkling waters of Spanish Lake.

Stretched out on the grass a few feet from the lake, Marty took a sip of lemonade. "There's a poem trapped inside me—I can feel it."

"Write it and gift it to the world," Hanna said.

"I haven't found the words to unlock it."

"What are you going to do?"

Marty stared at the cloudless sky. "The key is out there. I'm going to look for it."

"How can I help?"

Marty leaned over and kissed his girlfriend. "We'll search together and I'll let you know when I find it."

Hanna ran her hands through Marty's short blond hair. "I love poetry, particularly the Romantics like Keats, Shelley, and Byron."

Marty lobbed a small flattened rock into the lake, and said, "Keats walked woods like this and found his *To Autumn* and *Ode to a Nightingale*. He discovered *Ode on a Grecian Urn* in a museum. There's intensity within people born to be poets, and they find inspiration anywhere and everywhere. It's a gift from the heavens, or wherever your belief system takes you."

"Where and when do you want to start looking?"

Marty pointed. "We'll start with that cluster of gnats hovering over those purple azaleas. Are they just a bunch of swirling dots floating mindless in the air or is there a larger meaning to that picture? And what about honeybees searching the wild woods for anything sweet or when sunlight mixed with hot humid air bears down and makes life less comfortable. Are they expressions of truth only a poem can reveal?"

Hanna shrugged. "That's a tough question."

"Great poets like Keats and Shakespeare can taste rainbows, tame whirlwinds and whippoorwills, and shine special light on hate, envy, and happiness. I don't know if I've been blessed with those gifts, but I'm going to find out."

Marty, dressed in jeans and light-blue cotton sweater, grabbed the tan wicker basket and headed back up the leaf littered path with Hanna, leaving behind the melodic tones of clear cool water tapping the lake's bank.

While helping Hanna over a rotting log that blocked the path, Marty paused at the snap of a twig. They were being followed by a hungry-looking gray fox. He reached inside the picnic basket and pulled out a ham-on-rye sandwich and pitched it in the direction of the fox. After smiling at Hanna, Marty turned. He wasn't surprised the fox and sandwich had disappeared.

Later the path crossed a large patch of blooming red, purple, and shimmering white roses that sweetened the air with a dazzling perfume. While they gazed at nature's artwork, a gust of wind intervened causing the plants to shower multi-colored petals in every direction.

Marty poked around until he found the brightest ruby-red rose. After presenting the rose to Hanna, he said, "These flowers weren't here before. We must have taken a different path."

Hanna brushed the rose across her cheek. "This is the only path to and from the lake. Maybe we didn't take time to notice."

"Maybe we didn't."

The path widened as they approached a small clearing of neatly cut dark-green grass surrounded by majestic oaks, maples, and poplar trees in the prime of life. In the middle of the small clearing was a weather-worn park bench.

Hanna ran over and plopped on the bench. "Let's rest for a while."

Marty strolled onto the soft thick grass and sat next to Hanna. The odor of fall forest decay ringed this oasis of green. He pointed at three white doves circling the clearing. "That's a majestic view—above it all. But it's not meant for us."

A breeze swept in a minty scent while a box turtle lumbered past gripping what appeared to be a June bug. A moment later a light brown fawn on trembling legs approached Hanna.

Hanna elbowed Marty. "Where's the picnic basket? There are a couple of tomatoes left in there."

Marty stood and gazed at the trail. "I set it down when I picked that rose. It must be there. That's at least a half mile back, and it's getting dark and overcast. I wouldn't be surprised if we got rain soon."

Hanna shrugged as the fawn bolted into a nearby patch of evergreens. "Let it go."

"I'll buy you a new one."

"I got it for a couple bucks at a flea market. Forget it."

The clearing, including the bench, Marty, and Hanna, were suddenly immersed within a large white cloud spinning like an out of control merry-go-round. And then everything vanished.

"My goodness, what is this place?" Hanna asked.

Marty tipped the cabbie and then pointed at the sky-high tower. Embossed on the side of the building in large gold letters was 45 Rockefeller Plaza. Marty felt the allure, it whispered, "Step inside this special place—you'll be happy." It was all here—banking, boutiques, art, and delicacies of every sort.

"It's where people with lots of money come to play. I heard there's a restaurant up there where people are provided shovels to eat caviar served in five-gallon buckets," Marty replied.

"Wow! I'll bet that building holds plenty of poetic inspiration," Hanna said.

"Let's take a look."

Marty purchased two VIP Access tickets for sixty-eight dollars, and they headed up to the Center's observation deck to take in the big view of the city.

With hundreds of others, they stood on the 70$^{th}$ floor and gazed at mountains of mortgaged brick, steel, glass, and concrete pushing up and out in all directions. Over on 6$^{th}$ Avenue, a multi-story building exhaled waves of dark-brown smoke as fire ate through its top floors. A TV helicopter hovered above while people and machines scrambled below.

A small boy with his face pushed up against the observation window turned to his mother. "Do you think that fire knows it's attacking a building here in Manhattan?"

The boy's mother slapped the kid on the back of the head. "It makes no special difference just because it's Manhattan; all buildings look alike to fire. It's true; fire isn't choosy where it works or lives—or who it burns. Nothing and nobody is above it all."

The boy jumped as the top floor collapsed. "Gosh—did you guys see that?"

Right across the street stood St. Patrick's Cathedral and its colorful stained glass windows, bluish white Tuckahoe marble, and faded brick. Marty had read it had undergone a one hundred seventy-million dollar facelift.

On the elevator ride down, Marty tapped a young guy on the shoulder who claimed to be a city alderman, and asked him, "Who has done more for New York, God or this guy Rockefeller?"

The man shrugged his shoulders. "You definitely have to say Rockefeller."

When they reached the sidewalk, Marty said, "It's getting dark, let's head to Broadway. Maybe I can find my key there."

He and Hanna joined thousands of laughing, hollering, sweaty folks searching for restaurants, theaters, or nothing in particular. Cabs swerved and barked at each other and at the street flush with tourists, attorneys, accountants, artisans, and street vendors rushing home or venturing out.

At the corner of Broadway and West 53$^{rd}$ Street they encountered an elderly man in a black suit and gold tie leaning against a brick building waving a sign proclaiming in big red numbers "2 + 2 = 5."

Marty asked the gentleman, "How does that happen?"

The old man gripped the sign, and with a Russian accent, said, "It happens with blunt force salted with lies and illusions."

Marty thought a moment, and replied, "I get it. Truth is whatever the folks in power say it is and nobody better challenge it."

"Everyone must decide which side they want to be on. Orwell and Solzhenitsyn screamed warnings, but not enough have listened."

"I always choose truth. Fantasy is fine as long as you recognize it as such."

"Not to folks determined to promote make-believe worlds. When challenged by truth they send a mob to attack those promoting it." The old man pulled a flask from his jacket. "Nothing changes reality, but this dulls it a little."

"I wonder why so many people are afraid of what truth has to offer," Marty asked.

The old man took a drink, and said, "This fear or hate of truth didn't start now. A Roman historian named Salvian wrote in the fifth century after the Goths had been in Rome and the Vandals in Carthage, 'The Roman Empire is filled with misery, but it is luxurious. It is dying, but it laughs.' Salvian recognized a world crumbling when others couldn't or wouldn't. Unpleasant or unpopular truths have always been hard to face."

"Maybe we could fast forward that by fifteen-hundred years and say, America is filled with misery, but it is luxurious. It's dying, but it laughs and laughs and laughs."

The old man pointed in the distance. "See that skyscraper. The condos start at twenty million, and the ones on the top floors go for forty million and up. Inside that luxurious steel, brick, glass, and glitz are people who do nothing during the day but shuffle paper on Wall Street and pontificate about the problems of society—talking the talk. At night they go home to those multi-million dollar sanctuaries and pretend they're above life's lessons. When that gated tower gets dragged down they'll know $2 + 2$ really did $= 4$. Truth catches up with everybody. And that's that."

Marty nodded. "You can't be wise or a poet if you're not committed to truth. Writing slick couplets to promote ice cream and car sales or catchy slogans for righteous political movements make you a product propagandist not a poet."

The old man whispered in Marty's ear. "Without respect for truth societies descend into chaos and then totalitarianism—a world where nobody gets what they want but everybody gets what they deserve. Look it up."

Marty nodded. "By the way, whatever happened to Salvian, that Roman guy you mentioned?"

"They executed him."

Marty shook hands with the old man and moved on to the next corner where he and Hanna ran into an intoxicated woman in green sweatpants and red-flannel shirt yelling to passersby she could recite any poem written by a romantic poet. Marty requested *To Autumn*, and then dropped ten dollars into her plastic collection plate. The tipsy street artist, who went by the name Lady Byron, stepped on a wooden crate, cleared her throat, and then delivered an eloquent recital of Keats' inspired music. The small crowd applauded as she scooped up her plateful of donations and ran inside a nearby liquor store.

Marty clapped, and said, "It must be nice to have people care what you had to say two-hundred years after your death."

Near 7$^{th}$ Avenue and West 50$^{th}$ Marty gazed up as beautiful people and sugar plum fairies smiled, drank, and danced the night away on the sides of buildings, living and loving in vibrant red, blue, and purple light shows. It was an intoxicating pitch of high-definition make-believe in the big city—a never-never land where everyone stayed mindlessly happy. Marty questioned how much truth lay in this giddy display. He concluded little—if any.

Greasy griddle smells drew Marty and Hanna to a street vendor's cart. After finishing a couple of foot-long hotdogs with cheese, they found themselves in the balcony of the Grand Duchess Theater waiting for a stage performance of *Hamlet* to begin.

Marty surveyed the mostly empty theater, and then turned to Hanna. "Now that's a hell of a question . . . 'To be, or not to be?'"

Hanna leaned back in her chair. "They say suicide is a sin."

Marty nodded. "True, but the question fits a lot of things besides living or dying. It's about how you live. Do you fight for truth, or just fade away when things get too tough?"

"It does make you think."

"That's what all great poets do—make you think and see things whether it's through a keyhole or from the 70$^{th}$ floor."

Hanna rested her feet on the balcony railing. "Have you been thinking about that poem of yours?"

"It's moving along."

The theater lights dimmed as the performance began. A moment later everything turned dark and disappeared.

Hanna rubbed her gloved hands together. "Damn it's cold up here."

Marty exhaled frosty air as he leaned forward in the chairlift and studied the snow-packed mountain peaks. "It's a small price to pay for the view. We can almost touch the clouds."

A flock of Canadian geese flew about fifty feet under the lift, honking as they descended toward a large clear lake a mile from the ski lodge.

Marty and Hanna watched a group of skiers decked out in orange parkas and green stocking caps zigzag down the slopes kicking up jets of snow. Two snowboarders followed close behind. In an open field next to the lodge parking lot they spotted about twenty adults engaged in a fierce snowball confrontation. Over what, who knew—maybe a parking space?

Marty said, "After dinner we could build a snowman. We'll dress him in your red scarf, my blue stocking cap, and slide on a pair of black cloth gloves. He could survive and be happy for months up here."

Wailing sounds from a stand of evergreens drew Hanna's attention. "That's a lonely snow leopard."

"Not in this part of the world. I'll bet it's a hungry mountain lion planning to root through food scraps from the lodge. It has to eat like everybody else."

"That's fine as long as we're not on its menu."

Marty laughed. "Somebody has to pay that food bill. Nothing is free."

"Why did they invent the word free if it doesn't apply to anything?"

"To comfort people who don't or aren't willing to take the time to think. That covers a lot of folks these days. Even love and God's grace require investments in time, energy, and a prayer thrown in now and then. Free just sounds so damn easy, like picking apples from a forbidden tree. Trust me every free has a visible or hidden cost somewhere."

"It sounds like a misleading and even a dangerous word. Who uses it the most?"

"It's used to sell ideas that aren't really there—something for nothing. It's a politician's favorite dream word, and it works. That's why they never get tired of using it."

"Maybe they ought to ban the use of that word. They've done that with other words, and it works—more or less."

"Banning the word won't ban the idea. They would just come up with another word selling the same dreams or nightmares. The answer is to think, think, and think some more. Everything comes tagged with a price—even taking the time to think."

As the chairlift arrived at the platform, Hanna said, "Use your poem to explore that challenge."

"I'll think about it."

After dinner, Marty and Hanna stepped onto the lodge terrace and gazed up at the night sky ablaze with flickering stars, a passing comet with its tail of gas, and a bright full moon throwing reflected light on the surrounding snow-packed mountains and valley below.

Marty leaned against the concrete terrace's four-foot brick wall, and pointed. "There's the Big Dipper. Its seven glorious stars belong to the constellation Ursa Major. That's a light show nothing on earth can match. Other distant shining figures can be galaxies billions of light years away in space and time. And it doesn't end there."

"Who built it, and where does it end?" Hanna asked.

"Damn, you ask tough questions. Nobody knows for sure where it came from or where it's going. Maybe we find out . . . maybe we don't. The problem is we don't know what we don't know."

"We must know something."

"It's bigger than us, and yet we're somehow part of it. How important a part is anybody's guess."

"Anybody must include poets."

Marty nodded. "Poets feel, touch, and explore realities science can't measure. Can science explain winged horses, enchanted forests, or the magic of meeting cherry blossoms in the spring? Science is so limited."

"Maybe a poet is up there among the stars working on an answer right now."

A howl rippled through the icy night air as the echo of avalanched snow sweeping down a distant mountainside rumbled past.

Hanna said, "Forget about building that snowman, let's get back inside. It's warmer and safer there."

Marty took a deep breath while scanning a sea of cold white in the valley and surrounding mountains mixed with thousands of tree limbs bent with snow. As he reached the lodge door he glanced up at the sparkling jewels that dotted the night sky and was overcome with a sense of being wrapped within a single beam of blinding light.

Hanna lurched forward as the Jeep's right front wheel bounced in and out of a ten-inch rut in the dirt road. "Why are we in this God-forsaken place?"

Marty poked his head out the driver's side window. "When you're on a journey you have to be willing to go to challenging places."

The mid-day temperature on the dashboard read a scorching 110 degrees. They were five miles from the main road, and not a tree, not a bush, not even a healthy looking stick or weed lay in sight—just mounds of dead or dying soil.

Hanna shouted, "This road leads nowhere, and we're getting low on gas. Turn around and let's get the hell out of here before things get serious. This place scares me."

Marty pulled to the side of the road and tossed the keys to Hanna. "Wait in the Jeep while I look around. There's something out there. I can feel it. I promise to be back in fifteen or twenty minutes."

Hanna checked her watch. "You got twenty minutes and not one second more starting from now."

Marty, in white T-shirt, brown shorts, and tennis shoes, walked about one-hundred feet, looked back and waved, and then continued around the corner and down a small hill—disappearing from Hanna's view.

As he marched down the road sweat poured over Marty's forehead burning his eyes. His arms dripped while streams of lost fluid flowed down his legs. The oppressive sky torched the back of his neck. He'd better hurry.

Marty flipped a handful of dust in the air and it fell back to the ground. No wind to move it or breeze to help give it a shove. He glanced around the barren landscape and realized there was no help anywhere; everything was on its own. He reached into his pocket and discovered he had left his cellphone at the Jeep. Feeling flushed and a little dizzy; he gave himself a few more minutes and then would head back.

After wiping the growing sweat from his brow, he spotted a small shiny figure roughly two hundred feet from the road. He discovered it was a gold pocket watch lying next to a partially covered human skeleton. An inscription on the back of the watch mentioned the name Horace Pitkin. Marty knelt and scooped away some of the dirt and found a black rosary wrapped around the fleshless left hand. He examined the skull for signs of bullet wounds or other injury while wondering how long these bones lay here, why they were here, and whether they belonged to a Horace Pitkin or some other unfortunate bastard.

Marty shoved the watch and rosary in his pocket and said a prayer while standing over the bones, wishing this soul a successful journey. He committed to researching Horace Pitkin, and would tell the cops what he found. The brutal heat reminded Marty it was time to go.

On the way back, Marty thought about dying and if it made any difference whether it took place in a hospital bed, nursing home, at home, or here in the middle of nowhere. He concluded dead was dead . . . after that why should anybody care.

Marty slow-walked up the road; over the next crest was the Jeep, Hanna, and a jug of refreshing ice water. And then a drive back to civilization where a cold shower, a steak dinner, green grass, and a soft bed waited. His mind began to wander; he recalled Grandma having his picture taken atop a small pony and marching into church for his First Communion so many yesterdays ago. And then his first job, first car, first date, first time voting, first marriage. Life came with a lot of firsts and one last heartbeat. Oh, how time slipped away.

Dehydrated and exhausted, Marty reached the top of the crest. But there was no Jeep, no Hanna, no ice water, nothing but a deserted dirt road coupled with boiling heat and ravaged landscape. He wondered why she left as he slumped to the ground. He realized he had no one to ask for help or place to escape. And then he remembered the rosary; there was nothing to lose so why not go there. Hanna said this place was God-forsaken, but that might not include folks that wander in.

Kneeling with eyes closed, Marty held the rosary with his left hand and began reciting the Apostles' Creed. After a few minutes, forced by the relentless waves of heat baking his body, he lay on his back and continued praying. Floating in and out between prayers were thoughts of how death and afterlife might feel. He screamed at three mangy vultures flapping their wings and laughing as they circled overhead. He'd give anything for a cold drink of water.

Marty let go of the rosary about halfway through its chain of prayers figuring any further piling on wouldn't make a difference if help was destined. Otherwise let the elements and time finish what it started. It wouldn't be long either way.

Marty laid waiting until disturbed by loud clanging bursts of sound coming and going in alternating rhythm. Something compelled him to look at the pocket watch. The time displayed six-thirty A.M. The sound continued to beat louder and louder.

Marty opened his eyes and recognized the darkness. He turned and watched his alarm clock buzz at his six-thirty wake-up time, and then felt the warmth of covers and softness of his pillow. He smacked the off button and then lay facing the ceiling for a minute, gripping the sides of the mattress just to make sure this was real.

At six-forty he jumped out of bed, showered, shaved, and then hurried downstairs to breakfast with a smile displaying a sense of relief and urgency. He had something important to share.

Marty scrambled a couple eggs, buttered some toast, poured a glass of orange juice, and started the coffee maker. Twenty minutes later he sat at his writing desk with pen in hand staring at a blank sheet of paper.

After a drink of coffee and a drag from a cigarette, he leaned back in his leather swivel chair and pictured emerald-green hummingbirds dancing with bees while fairies and snow-white angels held hands and watched from nearby bushes and trees.

It was time to write that poem.

## About the Author

Hourston's other works of fiction include:

*Monsters on Trial*
What happens when America grants its mad, bad monsters legal rights? The answer is found in nine exciting short stories where Mike Hoffmann and his team battle vampires, werewolves, zombies, and other goblins—mostly in court. This book is available at Amazon in paperback and e-Book. It's also available at Barnes and Noble, and Kobo as an e-Book.

*Tales of the Deep State*
Travel from New York, to Washington, to California, to Utopia, Tennessee, and small town Missouri and learn who's really in charge out there and how they get and keep their hold on power. Meet the bad guys and the Americans that stand up to them. This book is available in paperback and e-Book at Amazon. It's also available at Barnes and Noble, and Kobo as an e-Book.

Hourston has master degrees in history (MA) and business administration (MBA) from the University of Missouri-St. Louis.

Made in the USA
Monee, IL
21 September 2020

42484751R00102